PUFFIN BOOKS

THE MAGIC OF THE LOST TEMPLE

Sudha Murty was born in 1950 in Shiggaon in north Karnataka. She did her MTech in computer science, and is now the chairperson of the Infosys Foundation. A prolific writer in English and Kannada, she has written novels, technical books, travelogues, collections of short stories and non-fictional pieces, and four books for children. Her books have been translated into all the major Indian languages. Sudha Murty was the recipient of the R.K. Narayan Award for Literature and the Padma Shri in 2006, and the Attimabbe Award from the government of Karnataka for excellence in Kannada literature in 2011.

Read More in Puffin by Sudha Murty

Grandma's Bag of Stories
How I Taught My Grandmother to Read and Other Stories
The Magic Drum and Other Favourite Stories
The Bird with Golden Wings: Stories of Wit and Magic
The Serpent's Revenge: Unusual Tales from the Mahabharata

The Magic *of* the Lost Temple

SUDHA MURTY

Illustrations by
Priyankar Gupta

PUFFIN BOOKS
An imprint of Penguin Random House

PUFFIN BOOKS

USA | Canada | UK | Ireland | Australia
New Zealand | India | South Africa | China

Puffin Books is part of the Penguin Random House group of companies
whose addresses can be found at global.penguinrandomhouse.com

Published by Penguin Random House India Pvt. Ltd
7th Floor, Infinity Tower C, DLF Cyber City,
Gurgaon 122 002, Haryana, India

Penguin
Random House
India

First published in Puffin by Penguin Books India 2015

Text copyright © Sudha Murty 2015
Illustrations copyright © Priyankar Gupta 2015

ISBN 9780143333166

Typeset in Cochin by Manmohan Kumar, Delhi
Printed at Thomson Press India Ltd, New Delhi

For Anoushka, who will always be my Nooni

Contents

Introduction   ix

1. The Family   1
2. Visiting the Village   14
3. Learning to Cycle   40
4. A Wedding in the Village   51
5. Ajji's Garden   71
6. The Story of a Stepwell   82
7. Picnic at Varada River   95
8. The Cow's Delivery   108
9. Varada Hill   116
10. An Unusual Rain   128
11. Is It a Stepwell?   136
12. The Excavation   170
13. A Send-off Party   194

Introduction

Thirty years ago, my daughter Akshata was a little girl who loved to play hide-and-seek with her friends. One day, I went for a shower after keeping my four gold bangles in a small wooden box. I then went to sleep in the afternoon. Once I woke up, I finished my chores and remembered late in the evening that I had forgotten to wear my bangles. When I opened the box, I found only two bangles inside.

Immediately, I started enquiring about the other two bangles with the people at home. Akshata readily told me that she had been fascinated by the box and had opened it to find the shiny gold bangles inside, two of which she took out intending to play hide-and-seek with them. To my horror, she didn't remember where she had hidden them!

I scolded her and then all of us searched the entire house. But the bangles were nowhere to be found.

After some time, I started feeling bad about reprimanding Akshata. So I hugged her and gave up searching for the rest of the day. Over time, I forgot about the existence of those bangles.

Thirty years passed and things changed. Akshata became the mother of two lovely girls — Krishna and Anoushka. During one of their visits to Bangalore, both the children were playing hide-and-seek when suddenly, I heard something smash to the ground in the living room. When I rushed there, I saw Akshata scolding her daughters for breaking a vase.

That vase was no ordinary one — it had been with us for the past fifty years. When it was new, we placed it in a corner and kept fresh flowers in it. Over time, we had replaced them with plastic ones. No matter how many houses we changed, the position of the vase had remained the same.

I felt really sorry for Anoushka, whom I fondly call Nooni. In her excitement she had hurried to hide behind the curtains and her hand had unintentionally knocked over the vase. Nooni was upset about getting caught and Akshata was angry because of the broken vase, but I was pleasantly surprised to see two gold bangles on the floor, shining brightly in the afternoon sun.

I picked up the bangles and examined their design. The two bangles on my hands were identical to the ones that had been lost all those years ago.

I smiled and looked at my daughter. 'Akshata, these are my old bangles! Do you remember hiding them when you were little?'

She grinned. 'Vaguely, but I remember you scolding me very clearly.'

I turned to Anoushka and hugged her. 'Good work, Nooni! You have found my lost treasure. These bangles mean a lot to me—they were handed down to me by my grandmother, and one day, I will give these bangles to you.'

Nooni was thrilled. She was proud that she had found something valuable!

That night, as I lay in bed with Krishna and Anoushka, I thought, 'When a child makes a mistake, it can turn out to be a lost treasure, or maybe an important discovery. Children are unbiased and can easily think out of the box. They have a lot of interest even in little everyday things because of their innocence.'

This simple incident inspired me to write this special book, which I dedicate to my beautiful granddaughter Nooni. She is the heroine of this book—bold, determined, sporty and always in search of new adventures.

I would like to mention a few people who helped me in this escapade.

First, I would like to thank Shrutkeerti Khurana, my terrific editor, for this book. I looked towards her just like I would see Nooni, and explained many things to her—things that are novel and fascinating to a city girl.

I also want to thank Udayan Mitra, Hemali Sodhi and Sohini Mitra of Penguin Books India, without whose constant pushing, I would have kept postponing the book to a later date.

Children, you are very important to me. It is your free spirit that always makes me think young and write more for you.

Sudha Murty
Bangalore, October 2015

The Family

Nooni was a twelve-year-old tomboy who loved all forms of physical activity—whether it was walking, climbing, jumping or hiking. She was a foodie, but wasn't interested in cooking. She was not fond of TV or cartoons either. Sometimes, she watched *Chota Bheem*, but only when her parents told her to do so. She didn't like surfing the Internet or playing computer games.

If she couldn't be outdoors, she preferred to read. Unlike most other girls, she didn't care about the clothes she wore or the way she looked. Her father, Dr Shekhar, bought her dresses, skirts, hairbands and girly accessories, but Nooni usually preferred wearing a T-shirt and leggings.

When she was younger, she had long, curly hair that her mother, Usha, used to insist on plaiting every day. But as she grew older, she opted to cut it so that it fell to her shoulders, much to the disappointment of her mother, who was proud of her daughter's thick, long hair. Nooni loved braiding her hair and tying brightly coloured bows at the ends of her two plaits. There was nothing Usha could do to change her mind. Once Nooni decided to do something, nothing could stop her.

Now, Nooni's real name was Anoushka, but everyone called her Nooni. It was easy to spell and Nooni liked it.

Today was a big day for her. She was a seventh-grade student of a CBSE English-medium school called Kendriya Vidyalaya in Bangalore and was about to get her yearly report! As soon as the teacher handed her the report card, Nooni closed her eyes and prayed to God in a last-minute attempt to bribe him into giving her a good rank. While she didn't care much for how she was placed in the class, she knew that her father was very sensitive about it and she wanted to make him happy. With hesitation, she finally opened her eyes and turned to the first page of her report card. Her eyes searched impatiently to see her rank in class. Finally, she saw a two-digit number—10. She had ranked tenth in her class. 'Oh, Dad is going to be disappointed today,' she thought.

Absent-mindedly, Nooni looked up and saw her friend Ramya jumping with joy. Immediately, she knew that Ramya had come first. Nooni smiled. She was happy for her friend and got up to congratulate her.

Soon, she was surrounded by her friends. Everybody was either talking about the rankings or their plans for the ten-week summer holiday. Some were going to attend swimming classes, while others were taking courses in art, music or dance. But Nooni's parents had other plans.

It was time to board the school bus. Nooni said goodbye to everyone and began thinking about her summer plans as the bus began the journey home.

After a few days, she and her parents were going to leave Bangalore and head to a holiday resort in Coorg. This was their ritual every summer. Nooni's mother took a ten-day vacation from her job as a bank officer and her father, a doctor and a physician, adjusted his schedule so that he could get away too. It was a hard task for him to take off from the hospital because of the increase in patient load during the summer season.

The three of them always went to a resort, which they booked at least six months in advance. On their prior trips, they had visited Kodaikanal, Ooty, Yercaud, Nainital and Manali, among others.

The places may have been different but the routine was exactly the same. They would check into the resort and buy a few things from a market nearby so that Usha could make them some breakfast, or if she didn't feel like cooking, they would eat in a restaurant. After a sumptuous meal, the three of them would go out for a nature walk and her father, who loved photography, would take pictures of everything they saw.

If the resort had a swimming pool, Nooni and her father would swim and laze on the pool chairs for the entire day. Occasionally, other family friends also accompanied them on the trip. Before returning to Bangalore, Usha and Nooni would buy souvenirs for their friends. Nooni had mixed feelings towards such a routine vacation—she didn't really love it but she didn't want to miss it either.

After they came back from Coorg, Nooni was going to join a summer camp where she would learn yoga, painting, swimming and pottery for a few weeks. By the time the camp was over, school would reopen.

Nooni would have liked to do something different and new. But she couldn't think of anything. Her mind wandered to her mother's parents, who lived in Indore. The city was a furnace in the summer and her family did not like to go there at that time of the year. However, her maternal grandparents usually came to Bangalore in the winter and spent at least ten days with them. Sometimes, Usha took Nooni for a week to Indore during the Diwali holidays. But Nooni never felt comfortable there. Though her family spoke Kannada at home, the main language spoken by the people in Indore was Hindi. Moreover, it was a little different from the Hindi she studied in school. Maybe that's why she didn't have any friends there.

Dr Shekhar practised in a nursing home. He was the son of a farmer and belonged to a small village called Somanahalli, which was located on the banks of the Varada river in North Karnataka. Dr Shekhar's parents still lived in the village. Every year during the Ganesha festival, Nooni and her parents would make the four-hour trip to Somanahalli by car, and stay there for a few days. Dr Shekhar felt uncomfortable in the village and always wanted to come back to Bangalore as quickly as possible. Usha, on the other hand, didn't mind spending time there. Nooni liked Somanahalli. It had huge fields, a sparse forest and big hills. She loved going with her grandfather to the fields every morning. There were plenty of vegetables and fruits for her to see, like rice, paddy and banana. At home in her grandparents' house, she was fascinated by the cows in the cowshed.

Still busy with her thoughts, Nooni realized just in time that the bus had reached her stop. She hurriedly got off and walked home. Her family lived on the fourth floor of a nice apartment complex in Jayanagar. When she reached home and rang the bell, Usha opened the door.

Nooni was surprised and happy to see her mother. 'Mom, what are you doing back from office so early?'

Without waiting for a response, she handed over her schoolbag to her mother and went inside the bedroom to change her clothes. On her way, she passed by the kitchen and saw the maid, Kaveri, cutting vegetables.

Usha followed her. 'Nooni, I am sorry. We are not going to Coorg this year. I hope you aren't too disappointed,' she said.

'That's fine, Mom. But why? What happened?'

'I have to attend a special training programme in Delhi. It is compulsory and I have to report there in a few days. The training is for six weeks, Nooni.'

'Oh Mom, I want to come to Delhi too! You know how much I love it there.' Nooni went to her mother and hugged her.

Usha knew that her daughter loved places with monuments, probably because Usha herself was a graduate of history and often told Nooni simple and short stories about famous buildings. A few years ago, Shekhar had been invited to speak at a four-day conference in Delhi, and Usha and Nooni had accompanied him. While Shekhar spent his days working, Usha and Nooni went to see the Qutub Minar, the Red Fort and Humayun's Tomb. Nooni was enchanted by the stories behind the old buildings.

'No, my child,' Usha said a little sadly. 'I can't take you. I have to stay in a shared room with another colleague. Also, Delhi will be very hot right now.'

'Hotter than Indore?'

'Of course!' said Usha.

'Then I will have to spend my entire vacation in summer camps,' declared Nooni unenthusiastically.

'No, that may not be necessary,' Usha said thoughtfully. 'Let me think about this a little bit and figure out where you can stay for six weeks. Give me some time. I will talk to your father.'

Nooni nodded. She was not worried. She knew that her parents would find a nice place for her to stay.

That day, her father also came home early from work. By then, Kaveri had finished cooking and left. Their routine was precise. Every weekday morning, Usha got up early to make breakfast and lunch for the family. The three of them ate breakfast, after which Nooni rushed to catch her school bus. Usha went to her office by scooter while Shekhar took the car to the hospital. Both the parents came back by lunchtime to eat together. Then, Usha would immediately leave and Shekhar would rest in the afternoon and go back to the hospital in the evening for consultation. He usually came back at night or sometimes even later, depending on the number of patients.

Weekends were a different story. Saturday was

a half-day for both mother and daughter. So Usha took Nooni swimming in the evenings. Sunday was the much-dreaded 'Homework Day'. While Nooni slogged, Shekhar would relax and meet friends or help around the house.

Kaveri came in the evenings every day, cleaned the house, cooked and left. Everything was like clockwork in their house and life. Nooni found it very boring.

At the dinner table that night, the subject of discussion was Nooni and where she could stay for six weeks. But even after a half-hour, her parents couldn't decide. After Nooni had finished dinner, Usha suggested, 'Why don't you go to the living room and watch *Chota Bheem*?'

Nooni understood that her mother wanted to distract her and went into the living room. Still, she could overhear her parents talking in the next room.

'Shall we send Nooni to Indore?' Usha asked her husband.

'No, she's not used to the terrible heat there. But it's also true that I can't look after Nooni by myself for six weeks. Maybe I should call my parents,' Shekhar wondered out loud.

'I don't think your parents will come here for

such a long time. As it is, your mother hardly stays here for a week before she starts having asthma attacks and then she rushes back home. You know they are uncomfortable in our small apartment, since they are used to living in their spacious house in the village. Still, I would like it if they agreed to come. Why don't you talk to them?'

'How about Dr Vivek's house?' Shekhar suggested. 'His wife and he can take care of Nooni. They are helpful, young and energetic.'

'Oh, that is not practical. They have a one-year-old baby and it is not right to leave our child in someone else's house for six weeks. It is better to talk to your parents,' said Usha.

Shekhar wasn't convinced. 'Can you drop out of your training programme?' he asked.

'No, I can't do it this time. I have already postponed it multiple times in the last few years. Now it has come to a point where I must complete the training if I want to grow in my career.'

Shekhar nodded, took out his phone and called his father. He explained the problem and requested his parents to come and stay in Bangalore for a few weeks. After he finished the call, Shekhar looked at his wife and said, 'Appa has a different opinion. He thinks that we should let Nooni stay in the village. They can't come now because one of the cows is pregnant and Aunt Sarasu's granddaughter is also getting married in the summer. The mango season will start soon and Appa says he has a lot of work. He's giving me every excuse that he can, not to come here.' Shekhar sighed.

'Don't say that,' Usha said firmly. 'Appa is not giving you excuses. He is telling you the truth. The cow, the wedding and the work in his fields are important to him. Just like I can't skip my training, your parents can't leave their home for six weeks either. But think about his suggestion. It may not be a bad idea for Nooni to stay in Somanahalli. It will be safe. My only concern is that she may not have friends there and if so, how will she spend her time?'

'Appa said that there is a new headmaster who has come to take care of the local high school. He has a son around Nooni's age. Also, many of my cousins' children are coming to the village for the wedding. I don't think that Nooni will get bored. Why don't we ask Nooni for her opinion directly?'

Usha smiled and nodded.

'Nooni!' both the parents yelled together.

Though she was still watching *Chota Bheem*, Nooni knew exactly what was going on. She wondered whether she should go to Vivek Uncle's house or to her grandparents in the village. In the end, she thought that it would be better to stay in Somanahalli because of the wedding in the family, the cattle in the cowshed, the vast fields that she could play in and the river that she could swim in.

She went to her parents and declared, 'I will go to Ajja's place.'

Usha heaved a sigh of relief, but remained a little concerned at the thought of sending her daughter away for so long. Shekhar was quiet.

'In that case, it is decided.' Usha turned to Nooni and said, 'We will sleep early tomorrow and the next morning, your dad will drop you to Somanahalli. You should both leave by six so that your father can get back to Bangalore the same day. I will pack your bags for the trip and a few things for Ajja and Ajji too.'

'That's a good idea,' said Shekhar. 'I will ask Vivek to come with me so that I don't get bored on the way back.'

Usha patted Nooni on her head and both of them headed back to the living room to watch the last few minutes of *Chota Bheem*.

Visiting the Village

Two days later, Nooni woke up early in the morning. She quickly had a bath and went to the dining room. Usha combed her hair and gave her breakfast. While Nooni was eating, her mother said, 'My child, this is the first time that you will be away from both Dad and me. I know your Ajja and Ajji love you very, very much but they are getting old. Try and help Ajji in the kitchen—maybe you can do things like washing the vegetables, cleaning the table, placing mats and filling the water.'

Nooni nodded absent-mindedly as Usha continued, 'I have packed your walking shoes, swimming costume and two pairs of flip-flops. I have also packed a few hats so that you can use them when you go out in the sun. Don't drink water from anywhere except for the boiled water that Ajji will give you. I have kept an extra water bottle so you can carry some water with you no matter where you go.'

'Don't worry, Amma,' said Nooni.

'I've added some fun books for you to read. Some of them are simple stories about the history of Karnataka and India. You can sit with your grandfather every day and he will add to those stories. I will call you as frequently as I can, but your dad will call every day. Behave well and enjoy your stay, Nooni. I don't want to hear any complaints about you. What do you want from Delhi? I will definitely get it for you.'

Nooni heard her mom's voice turn hoarse. When she looked up at her, she was surprised to see that her mother's eyes were moist. 'Get me whatever you like, Mom,' she said gently.

Usha patted Nooni's head.

When Shekhar walked into the dining room a few minutes later, Usha pointed to a basket and told him, 'Take these apples and oranges for your parents. I have bought two packets of walnuts and almonds for your father and two cotton saris for your mother. She will find them comfortable in the summer. Don't forget to give it to them now!

I have also kept some paper garlands for the local temple there. Your mother was looking for them when she was here the last time.'

Suddenly, Usha grabbed Nooni and gave her a long, tight hug before saying goodbye.

Nooni didn't understand why her mother looked so sad and simply hugged her back.

Vivek Uncle joined Shekhar and Nooni while they were putting their bags in the car and within minutes, the trio were on their way to Somanahalli.

Since Nooni was not used to getting up so early in the morning, she quietly fell asleep in the back seat. When she woke up, she found her father and Vivek Uncle chattering away about various things.

'I have a cousin who lives in Harihara near the Harihareshwara temple. We can take a bathroom break there if you want. Nooni can relax a little before we resume our journey,' Vivek Uncle suggested.

'Since there's barely any traffic right now, we may reach early if we don't stop on the way,' said Shekhar. Then he turned to Nooni and asked, 'Do you want to take a break to use the bathroom later? If so, we will go to Harihara.'

Nooni shook her head.

Shekhar continued, 'When I was younger, this journey used to take eight hours. I don't know how I survived it.'

'What was it like to grow up in Somanahalli, Shekhar?'

'Ours was a joint family of three brothers and their families. We all lived under the same roof. Both my uncles were older than my father and had four children each. My father, however, had only one child—me. So we were a total of nine children. My mother was a patient woman and since she was the youngest wife, the family made her responsible for all the cooking. My poor mother has spent her entire life in the kitchen! It was the same menu for breakfast every day—poha or upma. I didn't like either of them. Sometimes, though, there was dosa or idli. When I complained to my mother about it, she would try to pacify me by saying that individual requests could not be entertained in a joint family. It was very frustrating for me at the time.'

'Now I know why you don't touch upma at any of our office parties!' said Vivek.

'Not only that, I always ask Nooni what she wants to eat for breakfast. I have told Usha to make whatever she wants and not what is convenient for us. I really had a hard time so I know how it feels. Growing up, I had the same problem with clothing. While the girls had a little more freedom, all the boys had pants and shirts made of the same colour and material. It was like I had a uniform at home and in school!'

Vivek laughed heartily.

Shekhar did not.

Nooni finally understood why her dad took her to a fancy mall on her birthday every year and asked her to buy whatever she wanted. Though he would have liked her to buy a dress, Nooni usually chose leggings and a tee and he never forced her to change her choice.

'You must have had a lot of fun though,' said Vivek.

'To tell you the truth, I didn't like living in a joint family. Individual merit is usually never considered or appreciated in such a family. For example, I was very good at studies but my cousins were not. Still, we were sent to the same school. Later, my parents sent me to Hubli to study and I had to switch from a Kannada-medium school to an English-medium one. It was a big change and a tough adjustment but I fared well. Eventually, I completed my graduation from Karnataka Medical

College in Hubli and my post-graduation from Bangalore. After coming to Bangalore, I knew I wanted to live in a big city. There are just so many more opportunities there!'

'How did you spend your summer vacations?'

'Well, there really wasn't much choice. It is a sleepy village with a population of around four thousand. There was no summer school or workshops and so there was nothing much to do. Amma would make a lot of papads, which needed to be baked in the sun. So the other kids and I helped her by running up and down the stairs and spreading them out on the terrace. If it rained, we rushed to cover them with plastic sheets. She would also make multiple kinds of pickles so we had to help her with cutting the mangoes or chopping wood because of the rampant shortage of electricity. There would be all kinds of errands to run. Of course, we had helpers but still, if we didn't work, they didn't work either. I hated the chores. Instead, I wanted to read. My limited stock of new books would finish within a week during my holidays and we did not have a library in our village. So, one summer, my father gave me Kittel's Kannada-English dictionary, which I memorized. In those days, the illiteracy rate was very high so some villagers would come to me to help them write their letters.'

'Are you planning to gift Nooni a dictionary too?' joked Vivek.

'Yes, Usha has already packed a dictionary in her bag but it's not that hard. It is a children's dictionary.' Shekhar glanced at Nooni in the back seat. 'Are you completely awake now? Do you want to eat something?'

'No,' she replied absent-mindedly. She was thinking about starting work on that dictionary soon.

'You must have fond memories of your village,' remarked Vivek.

'Yes and no. Almost all my cousins have left the village and are in ordinary jobs. After their parents passed away, they wanted to sell their property and I bought it because my father didn't want to lose our ancestral land. Practically, it is really of no use to me because I have settled in Bangalore and I don't plan to ever move back. I don't have any friends there and I feel like a misfit. I don't like to see the dirt, dust and the bad maintenance in the village. There's also the frequent failure of electricity. Now, it is very difficult for me to live there. Usha doesn't seem to mind it so much. Maybe it's because her father was transferred to many states and villages during his career at the bank. But still, I know that the village is my parents' life.'

'Do you still have any relatives there?'

'Yes, I have an aunt called Sarasu. She is my father's sister and is settled there with her children and grandchildren. I don't think she's ever gone out of Karnataka. Then I have a cousin who owns a medical store and his son is an army officer currently based in Delhi. He visits once a year and I make sure that I meet him then.'

'What does your father do in the village?'

'Oh, he is a very busy man. He's a trustee of a temple and whenever a wedding takes place, he is called for the occasion and the newly-weds take his blessings. He has a few cows and insists on taking care of them even though they only supply one litre of milk every day. He also grows paddy and coconuts but spends more money on the labour and then donates most of it to the temples. He grows bananas and gives them away to all the village children. Sometimes, he sells vegetables too. He is very happy going about his business. Amma is another one. She can't make food for only two people—she cooks for at least ten. They have a few servants who do little work but are reliable, paid well and fed even better. Overall, I guess you could say that my parents lead a happy and content retired life.'

Nooni started thinking about Ajja and Ajji's house in the village. She had been there many times. Ajja owned a fifteen-acre garden on the outskirts of the village and adjacent to it were huge paddy fields. There was a small and beautiful rivulet flowing through the garden. Ajja had built a small guest house and a few houses for the workers to stay in. There was a wall around the garden but not the paddy fields. He called this his 'farm'. Nooni loved the farm. There was so much water and fresh air and so many trees—it was her dream playground for hide-and-seek.

It was warm by the time they reached the sleepy little village of Somanahalli. Shekhar's father was standing outside the house waiting for them, along with an unexpected crowd of people. The villagers had come to see the important Doctor Saheb who belonged to their village. At least ten patients were sitting on the side, awaiting a free consultation.

As Nooni got out of the car and looked around, she noticed that Ajji was very busy serving tea

to all the patients. She rushed inside to meet her grandparents and touched their feet. Ajji immediately hugged her and Nooni felt the warmth of her hug. From the corner of her eye, Nooni saw Mahadeva approaching them.

Mahadeva was an eighteen-year-old boy. His father was a clerk in the Gram Panchayat while his mother, Savita, worked in the kitchen and helped Ajji every day. The family owned a small piece of land. Mahadeva dreamt of graduating from college, increasing his knowledge about horticulture and starting a greenhouse or a nursery of his own. But he needed money for his schooling. Luckily, Ajja was sponsoring his education and Mahadeva was very grateful to the old couple. He stayed in Ajja and Ajji's house and took a bus to college every day. In the summer, his college was closed and he made sure that he was available the entire day to help Ajja and Ajji with their chores.

Mahadeva came and asked, 'Ajji, where should I put Nooni's bags?'

'You can keep it in the room next to Amma's,' Shekhar answered his question and introduced Vivek to his parents. Shekhar, Usha and Nooni always stayed in that room during their visits to Somanahalli.

'No,' said Ajji. 'Please leave it in my room. I don't want the child to sleep alone.'

'Oh, Ajji! I am used to sleeping by myself in my room back home in Bangalore,' Nooni said confidently.

'This is not Bangalore, Nooni. There is better air circulation in my room at night. Also, I can tell you a lot of stories before we sleep.'

Nooni smiled and nodded enthusiastically.

Mahadeva kept the bags and brought the fruits and other goodies from the car into the living room. Nooni saw a few children swarm around the goodies. She only knew one of them, a girl called Medha. The children were fascinated by the contents of the basket.

Ajja noticed Nooni's curious face. 'Nooni, you will have many friends to play with during your vacation this time. You already know your cousin Medha, don't you?'

'Yes, Ajja. She is Sarasu Ajji's granddaughter.'

Medha studied in the seventh grade in the local high school in the village. She was very fond of the arts and was exceptionally good at rangoli and nature sketches. She was shy and took time to make friends but she was very helpful and excellent at household work.

'Then there's Amit, who has come from Delhi and studies in Kendriya Vidyalaya there,' Ajja continued. 'He is Doctor Kaka's grandson.'

Nooni nodded. She knew Doctor Kaka. His real name was Prakash and he owned a multi-purpose store in the village. It was mainly a pharmacy that also sold newspapers, milk and other grocery items. Since it was the only medical store in the area, people who could not afford to go to a doctor would go directly to Prakash. They would tell him their symptoms and request him for advice and medicines. In time, Prakash came to be known as 'Doctor Kaka' even though he was not a real doctor. His son was a colonel in the army but despite his regular transfers, he managed to visit Somanahalli for a few weeks every year and ensured that his son Amit spent all his summer vacations in the village. He would say, 'It is very important for a person to know his or her motherland as well as their village to develop patriotism. Amit must know where he comes from.'

When Amit first came to spend two months in the village, he found it hard but he adjusted very quickly. Now, he stayed in Somanahalli without either of his parents. He knew Hindi very well. Most of the time, he could be found swimming in the Varada river or in his grandfather's pharmacy in the evenings.

Ajja pointed to a boy who was busy sifting through the fruits in the basket. 'See that boy?' Ajja asked. 'He is Anand, the son of our new school headmaster, Shankar, and he's in the eighth grade. His family has just moved here from Mysore. He is an intelligent boy and an avid reader. He also knows a lot about computers and other subjects, because the atmosphere in his house is very academic. Father and son discuss politics, history, physics and various other topics almost every day.'

'Is Shankar around?' asked Shekhar as he relaxed on a chair. Vivek was sitting comfortably on a sofa nearby.

'You mean Shankar Master? He must be in school at this time,' said Ajja.

'His wife, Gowri, is my friend's daughter,' Ajji added. 'So we have given the family the adjacent house to stay in. Anyway, the house had been locked for years.'

'What happened to the house on the other side?' asked Shekhar, recalling the empty houses of his two uncles.

'That is under lock and key. We use part of it as storage and a part is kept ready for guests to stay in. If there is a wedding in the village and people come from outside, they can stay there,' said Ajja.

'Why? Isn't there a wedding hall in the village?' asked Nooni.

'No, the concept doesn't usually exist in villages. Typically, the wedding is performed at home and the guests are accommodated in people's houses,' Ajja concluded.

'Appa, I am going to leave after lunch,' interrupted Shekhar. 'I must reach Bangalore today. Usha will leave for Delhi in the afternoon.'

'I have kept some bananas, tender coconuts, ten kilogram of rice and a hundred lemons for you to take back home. Also, take a few vegetables and mangoes from our garden. Everything is organic.'

'No, Appa! Please, I can't! I will be living alone now and I don't need so much. It will just get wasted. Getting the water out from a tender coconut is a big process in the city. I'd rather buy it from the vendor who sits in front of my hospital and gives it to me ready to drink with a straw. We still have the rice you gave us last time. Moreover, there is no one at home to make pickle out of these hundred lemons. Just ten will be enough for me.'

Ajja sounded sad when he said, 'It doesn't matter. You can share it with Vivek.'

'No, sir, it is really too much for me too. I can only take half of everything,' said Vivek.

'Well, the car is already loaded with the fruits and vegetables. Give the remaining to a temple nearby,' suggested Ajja.

'The nearest temple is quite a distance away. Appa doesn't understand the logistics and distances in the city,' Shekhar thought to himself.

Meanwhile, Ajji started laying down banana leaves on the dining table. Nooni remembered her mother's advice and rushed to the kitchen. 'Ajji, may I help you?'

'You are such a sweet little girl. Why don't you sit down and eat with your father?'

'Let me at least give everyone water,' Nooni insisted.

'Is the water boiled and cooled?' Shekhar turned to his mother and asked.

'Shekhar, don't worry. As a doctor's mother, I am aware of the importance of clean water. We also have a water filter at home,' said Ajji and started putting the water into the glasses on the table.

'I don't know how I used to drink water from the river when I was a child but the funny thing is that I never fell sick. Maybe the rivers weren't polluted then,' Shekhar wondered silently.

Ajji had made several dishes for lunch but Shekhar did not taste all of them. 'I will have a light lunch, Amma, or I will become sleepy and be unable to drive if I eat too much.'

Ajji was unhappy but she recovered soon. 'Be careful while driving. Don't worry about Nooni. She will have a good time here. I have already made plans for her. Every morning, I will involve her in the activities of the home and every afternoon, she can spend time with friends. Many children from different places are coming for the wedding. So Nooni will have fun meeting them. I have stitched a silk langa and blouse for her,' said Ajji.

'I am planning to take her for my morning walks and show her different animals and birds which she won't see in Bangalore. Tell Usha also not to worry about her. We will try to call her once a day,' Ajja assured him.

Nooni smiled to herself. Ajja was a talkative person and his morning walks could hardly be called morning walks. He talked to everyone he met on the road and leisurely took an hour to reach his farm, which was no more than a twenty-minute walk away. Then he would spend an hour there and bring back some vegetables and fruits to the house.

Soon, it was time for Shekhar and Vivek to begin their journey back to Bangalore.

Nooni hugged her father. 'Dad, I will enjoy myself here. Please don't worry.' She was happy to stay in the village. There would be no routine and no summer camp!

Shekhar smiled, opened his bag and took out a brand new cell phone. He handed it to Nooni and said firmly, 'You will never get this privilege in Bangalore. I have bought this for you but only for while you are here. The landline in Appa's house doesn't always work and I am quite certain that the reception here may not be that good either. You can use this to call us when there's proper network.'

'Can I take pictures with the phone, Dad?' asked Nooni excitedly.

'Yes, of course you can.'

Nooni did not know how to operate the new cell phone but she knew that she would figure it out quickly because even in Bangalore, she knew how to use her mother's cell phone better than her mother did. She was pleased at the thought of taking pictures of Ajja's farm, the cowshed and the fruits and vegetables.

Nooni happily said goodbye to her father and Vivek Uncle. As soon as the car left, she suddenly felt like she should have gone back with her father. For an instant, she felt abandoned in a strange place without her parents. Her thoughts were cut short as Ajji's voice called out to her, 'Nooni, I am eating lunch now. Come and sit next to me and help.'

Ajji's real intention was to distract her. She understood what the child must be feeling. Softly, Ajji said, 'Someday, you will have to leave your parents' house—either to study or because you are getting married. At first, you may find it difficult but you will learn a lot and eventually, you will adjust. Then you will find that it is a nice feeling to be on your own. Look at your father—he left this village when he was just sixteen years old, and when Ajja went on pilgrimages, I was left here all alone. But I learnt to manage the farm and the house. So when you go back to Bangalore after two months, you would have learnt and understood more than any book can ever teach you. Now, tell me, would you like to watch cartoons?'

'No, Ajji, I don't want to watch TV,' replied Nooni. Her eyes were focused outside the main door on a bicycle leaning against a wall. 'Ajji, who rides that bicycle?' she asked.

'That bicycle belongs to Anand. He rides it like the wind. In fact, every child in the village knows how to ride because the government gives all the students bicycles. Why are you asking? Don't you know how to ride?'

'No, Ajji, I don't know how,' Nooni said, a little disappointed. 'In fact, the government does not give bicycles at my school.'

'Maybe not. You are from a big city and a different school.'

'I also want to learn how to race with the wind, Ajji,' Nooni whined.

'It is not difficult to learn how to ride a bike.

I can ask Anand or Mahadeva to teach you, but remember that unlike Bangalore, the roads here are not tarred and you may fall. And if you are scared of falling, then you won't be able to learn. Why didn't you learn in Bangalore, Nooni?'

'There are barely any open spaces for kids like me to learn to ride.'

Just then, Anand, Amit and Medha walked in through the front door.

Ajji asked them, 'Children, did you all eat lunch?'

They all nodded and said 'hi' to Nooni. Amit added, 'But I haven't eaten any dessert.'

'I knew it,' Ajji smiled. 'Follow me. I have made payasam today from the milk our cow Basanti gave us. Nooni, please bring four bowls and spoons from the kitchen.'

Quickly, Nooni got the bowls and the spoons. Within a few minutes, the four children sat and ate their fill of the payasam without hesitation. Nooni felt a little awkward. In Bangalore, she would not behave so shamelessly in anyone's house — even if it was a friend's home.

Suddenly, she felt shy and didn't know what to say to Anand, Medha and Amit. After a minute, she mustered up her courage and turned to Anand.

'I want to learn cycling and Ajji said that you are very good at it. Will you teach me, please?'

Anand looked at her closely. 'But you are wearing a dress! Change into pants first and we'll go to the school playground. Also, don't blame me if you fall down. It happens. I fell down three times while I was learning. I can show you the scars right now.' He proudly lifted his shirt sleeves and rolled his pants up to his knees. He had three distinct scars.

'Anand, be gentle. Nooni does not have to learn cycling in a day. She will be here for six weeks,' said Ajji.

'When do you want to start?' Anand asked Nooni.

'Now?' It was a half-question.

Anand nodded.

Ajji called out to Mahadeva and instructed him, 'The kids are planning to go to the school playground. Go with them and keep an eye on all of them. Nooni is going to learn cycling so you can help her and ensure that she doesn't do too much in one day. In fact, you can teach her yourself. Come back before the sun sets. Here, take some apples with you in case the children or you feel hungry.'

Then she turned to Medha. 'You can also go and get your cycle.'

'Ajji, I need a cycle too,' said Nooni.

'Don't worry about that. You can take mine. I will bring it to the playground. I have something else I want to do anyway,' Medha offered immediately.

Ajji looked fondly at all of them. 'Children, whenever you want to go anywhere in the village with your friends, make sure that you take Mahadeva with you. He knows this area like the back of his hand.'

Nooni nodded obediently and rushed to the bedroom to change her clothes.

Amit said excitedly, 'Ajji, I cycle and ride a Luna inside the army campus because the roads don't have potholes and they are nice and wide. I will also bring a cycle.'

He turned around and ran home.

Learning to Cycle

By the time all of them reached the playground, it was almost 4 p.m.

Medha brought a cycle for Nooni and then went and sat on some steps a short distance away and immersed herself in knitting.

'What are you doing?' asked Nooni, walking over to Medha.

'I am knitting a small hanging purse. I saw the design in a book. It's going to come out very nicely.'

'Where did you learn to knit?'

'We have a weekly arts and crafts class in my school. Our teacher teaches us knitting, hand embroidering and needlework. I just love her class!'

A comfortable silence fell between the two girls as Medha continued to knit and Nooni watched in fascination.

After a few minutes, Medha asked, 'Your name is Anoushka, right? Then why does everyone call you Nooni?'

'When I was a small baby, I couldn't say Anoushka clearly. Whenever someone asked me what my name was, I would say Nooni. So my family and friends accepted my pronunciation and began calling me Nooni too. Somehow, the name stuck. But now that I'm grown up, people will look at me weirdly if I tell them that I can't pronounce Anoushka.'

Medha laughed.

Meanwhile, Amit and Anand started playing makeshift cricket on the other end of the ground.

Mahadeva shouted out from a distance, 'Come, Nooni. Medha's cycle is perfect for you. You can sit on the seat and your legs will touch the ground comfortably.'

'The most important thing about learning to cycle is getting the balance right,' said Mahadeva. 'The size of the cycle doesn't matter much. Now, hold the handlebar and start peddling. I will hold the carrier from the back so that I can keep the cycle in place and you won't crash to the ground. Don't be scared, Nooni. You will be fine. This is an open space and you won't hit anyone.'

As Nooni started peddling, she felt her heart sink. The cycle was wobbling! She could hear Mahadeva's instructions behind her.

'Continue peddling!'

'Go forward!'

'You're holding the brake, Nooni! Don't do that! You should never brake when you are going fast or you will topple over. When you want to stop, gently brake and the cycle will slow down just enough for you to put your feet on the ground, which will bring it to a halt.'

Nooni cycled almost a hundred metres with Mahadeva holding the carrier and running behind her. She was happy that she could pedal and move.

Mahadeva encouraged her, 'Keep going! This is a large ground. Take the cycle wherever you want. I will hold you.'

Nooni started peddling faster. After an hour, she was comfortable and started balancing on her own, even though she was a little shaky.

'Come on, let's go another hundred metres,' said Mahadeva breathlessly.

Suddenly, she heard laughter behind her. When she turned back to see what was happening, she saw Mahadeva grinning at her from a distance.

He was not holding the cycle anymore! For a few seconds, she was happy that she was able to ride independently but then her cycle started wobbling and she crashed with a thud.

Mahadeva came running to her and said, 'Never turn back, Nooni. Look ahead and ride.'

For two more hours, Nooni continued to practise. Sometimes, Mahadeva held the cycle and other times, he would get Nooni started and then leave her to ride alone. By late evening, Nooni could cycle a short distance without his help and without turning back.

A little while later, the children said their goodbyes and went back to their homes.

The next morning, Amit and Anand did not come to the playground. They didn't want to play cricket anymore and thought that it would be boring to watch Nooni cycle again. So they decided to go kite-flying. Medha also did not turn up. It was just Nooni and her teacher, Mahadeva.

Nooni practised relentlessly, obsessed with the task at hand. By the end of the afternoon, she was confident and could manage to cycle on her own.

Mahadeva advised her, 'Listen to my tips, Nooni. First, if you are going fast when you make a turn, then you will lose your balance. So when you want to turn left or right, slow down and then make the turn. Second, you should learn to balance while climbing uphill or coming downhill. Third, it is harder to cycle slowly than to go fast. It is best to try and keep a medium pace. If there are any potholes, go around them. Now you are ready to do this on your own. Go ahead and cycle. I will be back in two minutes.'

Nooni began cycling on her own. She felt free.

From the corner of her eye, she saw Mahadeva carrying a box. She turned the cycle towards him but she was too quick. She fell down and hurt her right knee. Blood started oozing out of the wound. Though it was really smarting, Nooni said bravely, 'Oh, it barely hurts! Don't worry.'

As Mahadeva came closer, she saw the box in his hand—it was a first-aid box. He smiled and without saying a word, made her sit on the steps nearby, washed the wound, wiped it clean with an antiseptic and bandaged it. He then grinned and said, 'I knew you would do something like this, little Nooni. That's why I went to bring the first-aid box. It is not hard to learn how to cycle. The trick to becoming a good rider is to fall less and control the bicycle well—that is very important. Today, I think that you have learnt around 80 per cent of the task. Tomorrow, I will sit on the steps and you will take ten rounds of the ground at a stretch and without falling. Then, I will get my cycle and come from the opposite direction to give you some practice on how to handle traffic. The day after that, I will put two kgs of dead weight on the carrier and check if you can still balance the cycle.'

When Nooni showed her grandparents the scrape on her knee that evening, they did not get scared or tell her to stop learning. Instead, they encouraged her, 'Falling down is a part of learning. You will be okay, Nooni.'

By the end of two more days, Nooni had completed Mahadeva's cycling curriculum. She fell down once more but she wasn't hurt much and just a Band-Aid was enough.

'Nooni, I have taught you the basics and you can do this on your own. You must continue to practise and maybe then you can even try cycling with one hand or with none at all! Excellence is not gained by accident, it is by habit,' said Mahadeva.

Nooni felt proud of her achievement. Now she could cycle all over Somanahalli and its bad roads without falling down. She started wondering about the things she could do in Bangalore with a cycle. Would her parents allow her to cycle to school? She didn't think so.

One evening, Nooni went to visit Medha at her house. Amit and Anand were also expected there. Medha was busy crocheting a tablecloth. She had a scrapbook near her where different kinds of cloths were displayed with various types of stitching. It seemed like an interesting book.

Medha's grandmother was very happy to meet Nooni. She asked, 'What time do you go to school in the city? How does your mother manage to work and do her chores at home?'

'My school is at 8.30 a.m., but I get up two hours earlier because I have to leave home by 7.15. I have a quick breakfast with Mom and Dad. Otherwise, I won't get to see them until the night. Sometimes, Dad comes very late from the hospital and by then, I am already asleep. We have a half-hour lunch break at school. My school closes at four, but I reach home after one and a half hours because of the crazy traffic in Bangalore.'

Medha piped in, 'My school is also at 8.30. But I leave home only fifteen minutes earlier because it's so close to my house. I don't even take the bicycle with me. We have an hour's lunch break so I come home and eat with Ajji and Amma. Then I go back to school and return home by 5 p.m. I help Amma with some of her chores for an hour, and then I do my homework.'

While they were talking, Amit and Anand entered and Medha's grandmother started serving them delicious snacks. There were gulab jamuns, murku, samosas, jalebis, biscuits and an unending supply of potato chips.

'What about your projects, Medha?' Nooni asked, recalling the stressful projects in her school.

'Our project work is usually done in school. If I have a problem, I ask Shankar Master directly, but our projects are not tough.'

'In Kendriya Vidyalaya, the teachers make all of us sit down and do the project work after class. We have a nice lab as well. But at school, we are like members of one family. Unlike other schools, we don't hide things or compete with each other. We share. That is the culture of the army,' said Amit.

'I don't have a problem with project work. Dad and I always discuss everything and he always has good ideas,' said Anand.

Nooni said, 'Project work in my school is hell. There's so much competition—who does the most difficult project, how many pages there are in the project report . . . and most of the time, parents do the work and credit their children. But Mom never does that. She says, "I will give you inputs but you do the research and do it yourself." Maybe that's the reason I never get good marks for my projects like my classmates. I have heard my parents say that the PTA meeting also sometimes turns out to be a competition among parents.'

Nooni remembered her father telling her, 'It is an extremely competitive world out there. If there are twenty vacancies for a job, then be sure that at least two thousand people would have applied for it. Unless you are at the top, you will not get good jobs.'

'But how is it possible for everyone to be at the top?' Nooni thought sadly.

At that moment, Medha's grandmother put a jalebi on her plate and Nooni immediately forgot about her thoughts.

A Wedding in the Village

The next day, Ajji woke Nooni up early in the morning. She said, 'Nooni, we have to go to Sarasu's Ajji's house today to help with the wedding preparations. There is a lot of work to be done. Get up and have a bath, eat your breakfast and then we'll leave. You know, when the village did not have electricity, my family worked from sunrise to sunset to work the maximum that we could in the daylight hours. That's how I got into the habit of getting up early and sleeping early too.'

Nooni yawned and stretched out her arms. 'What work do you have for the wedding, Ajji?' she asked sleepily.

'We are going to help with laddoos today and papads tomorrow. After that, we are going to make a lot of pickles for the wedding lunch. And

🌴51🌴

of course, we'll make some extra to last us through the year.'

'Why are you making everything, Ajji? Aren't there any sweet shops here? What about Haldiram's? In Bangalore, we always buy such things from MTR, Maiya's or Haldiram's. Mom doesn't makes laddoos, pickles or papads at home.'

'My child, your mother works full-time and in the big city where the apartments are small, there's really no place to store an entire year's stock. So the best way to get things is by buying small jars from the market. But in the village, you don't have any such shops. And the truth is that we have fun making these goodies.'

'Why do you want me to come with you? What am I going to do there?' Nooni wondered.

'Well, the ladies and I will do the main portion of the work but you and the other children must help us by running a few errands,' said Ajji. 'When your father was young, he also used to come and help me.'

Nooni nodded and went to the bathroom to get ready.

When they reached Sarasu Ajji's house, Nooni saw that the house was being whitewashed. She noticed that there were many children from the village. Everybody seemed busy. Some children were bringing ghee from the storeroom, some were busy washing plantain leaves and dabbas and others were cleaning the verandah. Suddenly, she glanced to the side and saw heaps and heaps of laddoos on the verandah. She had never seen so many laddoos in her life!

She saw Anand standing near the laddoos and looking at them hungrily. She went and stood by him. He licked his lips and said dramatically, 'Nooni, do you know how many laddoos they make? There are two laddoos for each adult and three for each child. On top of that, they make extras too! I'm so tempted to eat a few but my mother will get angry if she finds out.'

Nooni laughed.

The wedding was a week away. So Ajji and Nooni went to Sarasu Ajji's house every single day.

There were many people who kept trooping in from different villages and cities and they all stayed till the wedding was over. Some even stayed in the house next to Ajja and Ajji's home. Though Nooni didn't know many people, there were many girls of her age. There was a lot of noise and fun throughout the day in Sarasu Ajji's house. Many women volunteers kept coming in to help with some of the work. The back garden was converted into a makeshift kitchen. Breakfast and lunch were served at the house and there was a constant supply of tea and snacks throughout the day. A shamiana was erected. There were big carpets and mats everywhere. At night, the men slept in the verandah while the women slept inside the house after discussing food, saris and Sarasu Ajji's lovely gifts. The children had fun sleeping on the terrace under the stars.

Nooni felt awkward at the informality of the people there. She recalled Vivek Uncle's quiet wedding in Bangalore. It had taken place in a hotel and was very short—just about half a day and without many rituals. She also remembered a wedding that she had attended with her parents at the Bangalore Palace. The palace was completely lit and there were thousands of people walking about everywhere. There was a parking problem and a big line for the reception. There were plenty of food stalls, including chaat, Thai food, North Indian food and South Indian delicacies. People were more interested in eating the food than the actual ceremony. Unlike the happy wedding at Sarasu Ajji's house, Vivek Uncle's and the Bangalore Palace weddings were boring.

Finally, the wedding day arrived. Ajji wrapped herself in her best silk sari and Nooni wore a red blouse and the yellow silk langa with the red border. Ajji gave her a necklace to wear but Nooni didn't like it. Still, she wore it to make Ajji happy. From morning till evening, Ajja and Ajji were busy with the wedding activities. Since they were old and respected in the village, everyone who attended the wedding came and touched their feet. Ajji showed off Nooni to everyone. 'This is my granddaughter, Anoushka,' she said to whoever she met. 'She has come from Bangalore to spend the summer with us.'

Nooni felt a little shy.

The variety of food was definitely not as diverse as in Bangalore, but it was tasty and traditional. Lunch was served on plantain leaves. Sarasu Ajji told all the women, 'Please make sure you pick up a box of mithai from the table on your way out.'

After lunch, Ajji went and stood at the table near the exit and Nooni became her assistant. Boxes of mithai were piled up on it. Ajji held a silver bowl

with kumkum and offered it to all the women while Nooni handed a mithai box to the families as they made their way out.

That night, when the trio returned home, nobody wanted to eat because they had had lunch at four in the afternoon. All three of them were very tired, so they went to bed early.

'Ajji, tell me a story,' Nooni insisted once the lights were off.

'Nooni, aren't you tired? I'll tell you a story tomorrow.'

'No, Ajji, I want to hear a story now. Ever since I have come to the village, you haven't told me even one story,' Nooni persisted.

Ajji got up and pulled the curtains aside. It was a full moon night and the moonlight came through the window into the room. 'It's as if a magic lamp has been switched on,' thought Nooni.

'I don't see such bright moonlight in the city or in our house, Ajji. How has the moon lit the entire bedroom?'

'You live in an apartment. Your bedroom faces another apartment complex and all the streetlights are on in the night. Then how will you see the effect of natural light in the city? Here, we have very few streetlights and there aren't any high-rise buildings. My room faces the garden where there's open space and windows for the light to come in easily.'

'Ah, now I understand, Ajji! Tell me a nice story about the moonlight then. I know you have a story for every occasion,' grinned Nooni.

Ajji smiled and said, 'Of course. What I'm about to tell you happened a thousand years ago in this very village.

'Long, long ago, there lived a handsome king named Somanayaka. He was brave, kind, courageous and very generous. His kingdom lay in the delta between the rivers Varada and Tungabhadra. There was a thick forest around the area and many wild animals lived there. Sometimes, they would enter villages and scare the people, destroy the crops and eat the cattle. After a number of such complaints and no improvement in the situation, the king decided to hunt these wild beasts himself. Two days later, he went hunting on his horse with his soldiers by his side. Soon, he had left his soldiers far behind and lost his way.

'The day passed and turned into late evening. The king's horse became tired and Somanayaka tied him to a tree and went in search of food. He collected some fruits, ate them and brought some grass back for his horse. Suddenly, he felt very sleepy. It was a full moon night and the breeze was cool and pleasant. Somanayaka noticed a flat rock behind some bushes and decided to rest. Within minutes, he was asleep. Suddenly, he was awakened by the sound of girls chatting. He opened his eyes and glanced at the sky. To his surprise, there was a ladder coming down from the moon which joined some stairs that went all the way from the moon to the Earth. A group of beautiful women were coming down the steps. They all wore white saris and pearl ornaments and carried golden pots at their waists. He squatted near the bushes and counted them — they were seven in all. He wondered what they would do next.

'As soon as they reached the Earth, the oldest woman touched the ground with a stick and he saw the ground give way and open up. All of them slowly disappeared inside the ground. Somanayaka was not scared but he was desperate to know where they had gone. Carefully, he came out of the bushes and peeped. Then he felt a little bolder and walked towards the big hole in the ground.

He was surprised to find himself looking into an enchanting stepwell!'

'Ajji, what is a stepwell?' Nooni asked.

'It is a well that has steps inside so that it is easy to get to the bottom. There are many stepwells in our country. In fact, some of them are very famous. Remember that picture of the well you sent me from your trip last year to Abhaneri near Jaipur?'

'Oh, that's true. There was a huge well there with almost three thousand steps. Are you talking about something similar?'

'Yes, I haven't seen Abhaneri myself and the one that Somanayaka saw was a small stepwell. It had only twenty-one steps. But there were seven small exquisitely carved Shiva temples inside the well. Somanayaka looked down and observed the stunning carvings and pillars and the beautiful angelic women. He enjoyed seeing them play hide-and-seek for some time. Then they filled their pots with water, poured it on an idol of Lord Shiva and performed a puja. The whole process took several hours. By then, the sky started getting lighter as it was daybreak and the moon started fading. Somanayaka hid behind the bushes again. Soon, the women climbed the steps and went back to the moon. The steps disappeared and the ground closed up.

'Somanayaka sat in the bushes for a long time. Suddenly, he felt confused. Had it been real or had it all been a figment of his imagination? Did he really see the ground open up and a well underneath? He stood up and came out of the bushes. He searched everywhere for a sign of the well but with no luck. There was not a single remnant of the incident he thought he saw. "I must have been so tired that I slept off . . . and had such an elaborate dream that I thought that it was real," he said to himself. He turned and started walking back to his horse. Suddenly he saw something sparkling on the ground—it was a broken pearl necklace. Somanayaka collected all the pearls and realized that it hadn't been a dream after all.

'He tried to recall if he had ever heard about a stepwell in his kingdom but nothing came to mind. By then one of his followers had traced him and come to his rescue. But Somanayaka told him, "Go back and inform everybody that I am safe. I will stay here for a few days. Give me your food ration before you leave. I know the route and I will come back on my own."

'The next day, he waited near the bushes again, but nothing happened. He waited for one more day and still, the women did not appear. After another uneventful day, he thought of other possibilities, "Maybe these beautiful maidens come only on full moon days."

'Keeping that in mind, he got on his horse and went back to the capital. He met the royal astrologer and found out the date of the next full moon night.

'When the night came, he waited behind the bushes and this time, he was not surprised when the ladder came down from the moon. He knew the whole process by now and looked forward to the puja of Lord Shiva. Somanayaka was an ardent devotee of Lord Shiva. After the puja, he decided to take a chance and meet the maidens. Boldly, he came forward and stood near the stepwell. "Beautiful maidens, please don't be alarmed. Here's my pranaam to all of you." He folded his hands together and continued, "You have chosen our land for your worship of Lord Shiva and I am really grateful to you. I have noticed that when you go back, the ground closes on its own. May I earnestly request you not to make the well disappear? Please keep it open so that everyone can worship Lord Shiva in this beautiful ambience."

'The women looked up at him in fright. It was a rude shock for them to see Somanayaka there and they gathered closely together. Then the eldest maiden took the lead and said, "Who are you? Why have you been observing us without our knowledge? This stepwell was built by a great architect of the celestial heavens. It can't be used by the selfish people of Earth."

'Somanayaka bowed his head and said, "My sisters, I am Somanayaka, the ruler of this land. I know that this holy stepwell couldn't have been made by human beings. But Lord Shiva is fond of all his devotees, isn't he? Please grant me my wish. If you have any conditions, please tell me and I will fulfill them."

'The maidens spoke to each other in hushed whispers. Then the eldest one said, "We are impressed by your humility and your prayer. The water here tastes like nectar. That is Earth's specialty. Even though we live in the celestial world, the water there isn't as tasty as what we get here. So, we come every full moon night not to take a bath or spoil the well but to just drink and enjoy ourselves.

As long as you promise me that you will not dirty the premises and that this water will be used only for drinking, we will leave it as it is. People of your land can come and worship and take the water but before entering the stepwell they must take a bath and wash their feet. If your people do not follow the rules, the well will disappear along with your kingdom. Think about it. It is a big price to pay. Are you ready to take the risk of losing your kingdom?"

'Somanayaka thought for a minute and said confidently, "A source of water is a source of life. I will ensure that all your conditions are taken care of."

'The maiden continued, "We have one more condition. On full moon nights, the temple must remain closed so that we can continue our visits here. Nobody must be allowed inside to observe us or talk to us. We want our privacy to be protected."

'Somanayaka agreed. He stepped forward and gave back the necklace to the maiden. He said gently, "I think this belongs to one of you."

'The women were very happy with his honesty. They drank the water, climbed the steps and vanished. The stepwell remained where it was.

'Somanayaka went to the nearest water body to have a bath and then he entered the stepwell for the first time. It was much more beautiful from up close. When he reached the bottom, he cupped his hands and drank a sip of water. It was very tasty. He felt that it was better than nectar, which he had never drunk before anyway.

'The next day, he came back to the kingdom and proclaimed, "There exists a beautiful stepwell of Lord Shiva in our kingdom. People who would like to go there and perform puja can do so but on one condition—they have to bathe and cleanse themselves before entering the stepwell. The water there will be used for no other purpose except for drinking. Everyone can carry away one pot of water and no more. These rules are to be strictly followed and there will be no exceptions. The temple will remain closed on full moon nights and nobody will be allowed inside."

'Somanayaka wanted to make his people comfortable so he ensured that there was another water body for them near the stepwell. There, people could bathe, change their clothes and then enter the stepwell. The news spread like wildfire. People came from all over the kingdom to see the

architectural masterpiece and pay their respects to Lord Shiva. The well remained open on all days except on full moon nights.

'Days passed and word spread. People started coming from far and wide and from different lands. A small tourist spot was set up near the stepwell and named Somanahalli.

'Despite the increase in the number of visitors, the well was kept clean and guards monitored the premises around the clock.

'After some years, Somanayaka married a lovely lady—Queen Ratnavati. She was beautiful and courageous but headstrong. Somanayaka told her about the way the well had been discovered and how the celestial maidens had agreed to his request. Ratnavati wanted to know whether the maidens were more beautiful than her or not but she knew that she would never get a chance to meet them because they came only on full moon nights when no one was allowed inside the temple.

'One day, the king had to go to an important event in the neighbouring kingdom. Ratnavati told her husband, "I am not feeling very well. I think that I will stay back in the palace."

'The naive king believed her and departed for the event. As soon as he left, Ratnavati called for her chariot and headed towards the stepwell. She thought to herself, "I am the queen of this land. Every inch of it belongs to me. So what if the well is a gift of the maidens? The well exists on my land and I am the legal owner. My husband doesn't want to take a risk and obeys those maidens' words without question. I want to show him that nothing will happen if we break their rules."

'When the charioteers reached Somanahalli, the officers stopped her and requested, "O Queen. Please don't visit the temple today. It is a full moon night and as per the government rules, no one is allowed to go inside. Why don't you stay in the guest house tonight? You can visit the well tomorrow."

'Ratnavati did not listen to them. "How dare you stop me? I am the queen. Everything is under my control."

'Without another word, she barged into the stepwell. Since it was a full moon night, the entire complex was shining like silver. The water was shimmering and looked irresistible. She went into the water to bathe. Suddenly, she heard a noise. When she turned, she saw seven women standing on the steps. Though her heart told her that they were more beautiful than her, her ego did not allow her to accept the truth. When the maidens saw Queen Ratnavati in the water, they became upset. "Who are you? How dare you come here today? Has King Somanayaka forgotten our conditions?"

'Arrogantly, Ratnavati replied, "I am his queen. This land belongs to us and I make the rules—you can come the day I want you to visit. You can't tell me when I can and can't come here. The water here is the way it is because of the Earth and not because of anything you did."

'"Who are you to talk to us like this? You have not only disobeyed our rules but you have also dirtied the water. Once someone has bathed in this water, no one can drink it again."

'The women turned to leave. While going up the steps back to the moon, the eldest maiden said, "Rani Ratnavati, you are going to regret this."

'They climbed the ladder and vanished. Queen Ratnavati tried to get out of the water to go behind them and talk to them but all her efforts were in vain.

'Suddenly, there was thunder and lightning, followed by a huge gust of wind and rain. Ratnavati quickly climbed up the steps of the well. The earth quaked and within a few seconds, the well closed.

'The queen was scared. She had been warned of the consequences—she was going to lose her kingdom! She cried to herself and said, "I should not have done this. I have polluted the water and disobeyed my husband. I have destroyed my kingdom because of my arrogance."

'Somanayaka never came back from his travel and Ratnavati went mad crying in the streets. After a few days, nobody heard from her again. The kingdom was eventually abandoned. It was sad that the queen, who should have been the protector of her kingdom, had destroyed a precious water source, disobeyed royal orders, broke a promise and caused such a catastrophe.

'People say that our village, Somanahalli, is near the location of the stepwell. This story has been passed down from generation to generation but no one has actually seen the well.'

Ajji finished the story. Nooni looked at the moon with sleepy eyes, waiting for the maidens to appear.

Ajji's Garden

When Nooni woke up the next day, Ajji went into the bedroom and said, 'Don't rush off for a bath today, Nooni. I want to oil your hair and then wash it. It will take some time. So change into an old dress and come outside. We will sit in the front garden.'

Ajja and Ajji's house was located on a one-acre sized plot and it was surrounded by coconut trees and a huge garden at the back and in the front. There was a well and a pump used to water the garden through all the seasons.

Lazily, Nooni trudged to the bathroom and brushed her teeth. She didn't understand why an oil massage and a bath was such a long process here in the village. In Bangalore, she usually had a bath by herself. Sometimes, Mom would give her an 'oil bath'—she would quickly apply coconut oil on Nooni's body, give her a light massage followed by a bath. Usha was scared that if she used a lot of oil on Nooni, then the lines on the bathroom tiles would retain oil and become slippery. So Kaveri would clean the bathroom immediately after Nooni's bath.

Nooni changed her clothes and came out to the garden. She saw Ajji already sitting on a bench holding a bottle of greenish-black oil that had dark leaves floating in it. 'Come,' said Ajji. 'Sit here with your back towards me. I will massage the roots of your hair with this special oil. After the massage, don't wash your hair for an hour.'

'What's so special about this oil, Ajji?'

'Let me tell you an important secret. In our family, we make most of our treatments and medicines at home. For example, this oil contains leaves from the Brahmi creeper and other herbs from my garden. It also has camphor and powder from a red sun-dried hibiscus flower. Look at my hair.' Nooni turned around and Ajji proudly touched her thick and long hair. Though Ajji was old, her hair was not yet completely grey—it was more pepper than salt.

Ajji smiled. 'This is my mother's recipe. She used

this oil to massage the heads of all the girls in the family.'

Nooni sat quietly and Ajji continued, 'Nooni, there was no doctor or pharmacy in the village in the old days. So when someone was unwell and had symptoms like fever, cough, headache or body ache, they turned to home remedies. That's why we grew medicinal plants at home. Have you had a closer look at my garden and the backyard?'

Nooni knew that Ajji grew flowers in the front and some plants in the backyard. Other than that, she hadn't bothered to learn more. She looked around the garden and saw flowers of different colours. There were no gladiolas or gerberas but plenty of other native flowers like multiple varieties of jasmine, rose, champak and many more.

Ajji commented, 'I have a variety of jasmine that blooms every day. It is called nitya malige. Some jasmines bloom only in the summer like dundu malige while others like jaji malige have a reddish-coloured petal at the back of the flower and they bloom only in the evening during the rainy season. Then I have a really small variety of jasmine called suji malige—their stems are as thin as a needle, but their aroma is heavenly. Then there's kakada

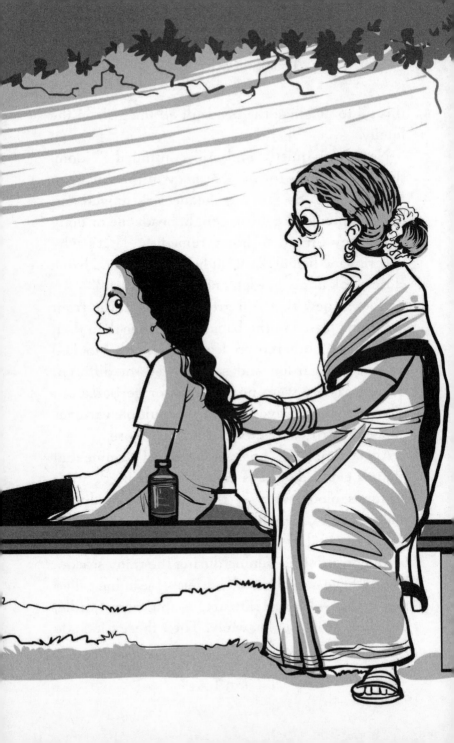

malige whose bushes produce buckets of flowers in the winter but without any aroma. Similarly, there are different kinds of champaks such as the small, highly fragrant ones called china sampige, the seasonal big and beautiful sampige that are local to Bangalore, and coloured champaks called kenda sampige.'

'Ajji, I can see roses in your garden too.'

'The roses that grow in Bangalore are much better, Nooni. Unlike our native plants, the rose bush is sensitive and needs a lot of care. Since we get too much sun here and the land isn't ideal for roses, we can't grow too many of them in the village. I have a few rose bushes but you can't compare them to the quality of flowers in Bangalore.'

'I attend the Lal Bagh flower show in Bangalore twice a year. They have a lovely rose garden that displays roses of multiple colours,' Nooni recollected. 'Ajji, what do you have in the backyard?'

'There is a bush called manoranjan that gives greenish-yellow flowers and another bush named raat ki rani whose flowers bloom only at night. Their fragrance is unmatched. People say that snakes are enchanted by the aroma of these flowers and they coil themselves around the bush at night.'

'Really?' Nooni remembered the snake she had seen in the zoo and became petrified. 'Snakes come and coil themselves here? In your home? Your room is so close to the garden, Ajji. What if the snakes come inside? We should start shutting the windows at night.'

Ajji laughed heartily. 'Nooni, snakes come wherever there are trees and bushes. They don't really come for the aroma, though people tend to believe in such stories. The real reason they come is to hunt for prey such as mice, because mice eat fruits and seeds. There is an ecosystem at play around and one animal depends on another one for its food and survival. Don't be scared.'

'Will you show me all the flowers, Ajji?'

'Yes, I will.'

'What else do you have?'

'The rest are all medicinal plants, Nooni.'

'You keep saying that, Ajji. What do you mean by medicinal plant?'

'Well, there are some bushes, trees and creepers whose leaves, stems, fruits, seeds, flowers or roots carry medicinal value. Your father tells me that a lot of tablets and medicines are made from the material extracted out of such plants.'

By then, Nooni's massage was over. She could smell her hair and its nice fragrance. Ajji tied her hair with a rubber band and said, 'Wear your slippers and then I'll take you to the back.'

In the backyard, Ajji started giving Nooni a tour of her plants. Nooni sensed her grandmother's pride—it was the same way Nooni felt when she won a trophy and took it home to show her father!

Unlike the front garden, there were hardly any coloured flowers in the back. Ajji showed Nooni a small bush with a lot of green leaves. 'This is tulsi.'

'I know a little about tulsi,' Nooni replied with confidence. 'Mom keeps a tulsi plant near the kitchen and waters it every day. But what is so special about this plant that everyone wants to keep it in their house?'

'My dear, it is of wonderful medicinal value and is used in plenty of home remedies. There are seven varieties but I only have a few in my garden. See this Krishna tulsi—it has dark leaves, Vishnu tulsi has pale green leaves, Ram tulsi has big, pale-green leaves and Kasturi tulsi has a wonderful fragrance. Then there's Ganga tulsi which grows mostly in cold areas such as the Himalayas. Its specialty is that it smells like tulsi but has unique leaves.'

'Then how did you manage to grow it here, Ajji?' Nooni asked.

'When I went for a pilgrimage to Gangotri, I brought the seeds back. Then I planted them in a pot, kept it in a shaded area and watered it frequently. So the plant has grown, but it is not as good as it can be. After all, it is not a native of our land.'

'What do you mean a native of our land?'

'Nooni, every terrain has a different environment with various seasons. So certain types of trees, bushes and creepers grow easily there compared to others and those plants are known as being native to the land. For example, you can't grow apples in the south. Similarly, you can't grow coconut trees in the north.'

Ajji continued and pointed out to a plant, 'Look at this creeper called amritaballi. It is excellent for fever and body ache. We pluck the leaves, boil them and then drink the water. See this brahmi creeper? It is used for hair oil. And here is the wonderful turmeric plant.'

Ajji stopped next to it.

'Oh!' Nooni exclaimed. 'Its leaves are green but turmeric is yellow in colour.'

'Silly girl, almost all plants have green leaves. Turmeric stays inside the earth as a bulb. When it is ripe, the leaves of the plant become dry. Once that happens, I take it out from the ground, dry it, sunbake it, process and powder it. Only then does it turn yellow. Whenever you have a cough, you can boil a little turmeric in milk and drink it.'

Nooni walked a few steps further, close to a bush with thin, green leaves and yellow flowers. Absent-mindedly, she plucked one of the leaves and put it in her mouth.

Ajji changed her tone and said firmly, 'Child, you can't just eat any leaf without knowing what it is. It may be poisonous!'

Nooni immediately spat the leaf out. 'What did I eat, Ajji?' she asked, looking a little worried. 'It has a strange taste.'

'This is the Nagadali bush. It is used for treating snake bites and as a snake repellent.'

Nooni nodded quietly. Then she pointed to the side, 'What is this weird grass, Ajji?'

'It is a special grass called lemongrass. We use it to make healthy green tea. I have other types of grass too, such as rice grass, which is used to give a fresh aroma to cooked rice. There's medicinal grass too. When our cows have overeaten or when their stomachs are not okay, I mix the grass with their hay.'

'Ajji . . .'

She was interrupted quickly. 'I think you've explored enough for today, Nooni. Come, let's go to the bathroom for your oil massage,' said Ajji.

'Please don't put too much oil. I don't like it.'

Ajji smiled and took Nooni inside her big bathroom—it was the size of a bedroom! There was a big copper pot embedded in the wall and a fire was burning below it. Nooni could see the remnants of dry twigs from the garden and the coconut trees.

Ajji made her sit on a wooden stool and said, 'Our body needs oil but that doesn't mean that you have to apply bottles and bottles of cream. Just a good rub with sesame or coconut oil and a good massage will relax your body. I won't use much hot water for your bath since it is summer.'

Without waiting for a reply, Ajji started massaging Nooni's body.

Though it was uncomfortable at first, Nooni liked the massage after some time. A silence fell in the bathroom. After Ajji finished, she asked, 'Child, do you want to eat something unusual?'

Nooni nodded enthusiastically.

Ajji washed her hands and brought a basket of

big seeds from the next room. She said, 'These are jackfruit seeds from the garden.'

Then she picked up a seed with a poky twig and rotated it in the fire.

'Ajji, be careful. You will burn your hand,' warned Nooni.

'Don't worry. I am used to this. The fire is on slow flame.'

Soon, she removed the seed from the fire and discarded the burnt covering. Then she gave it to Nooni to eat. It was delicious! Nooni had never tasted anything like it before—she was in awe!

'I want to eat more, Ajji,' she asked.

'Let's finish your bath and then you can eat more of these with some salt and chili powder or ghee with jaggery. Your father says that these seeds contain a lot of proteins but we only get to eat them during the jackfruit season.'

Ajji filled three buckets of water.

Nooni said, 'I don't think I need so much water, Ajji. Oh! I forgot to bring the shampoo from my room.'

'You don't need shampoo. I have shikakai powder, which will be enough. It will remove all the oil,' said Ajji and started pouring warm water on her head.

The Story of a Stepwell

The next day, Ajja set out for the farm with two helpers in tow. It was mid-morning and the sun was shining brightly in the sky. Ajja and his helpers were planning to pluck pumpkins and then head to the nearest town to sell them. Nooni stood on the verandah and called out to him, 'Ajja, I've finished my breakfast. I want to come with you to the farm too.'

'Child, it is hot and we will take a lot of time to finish our work.'

'That doesn't matter, Ajja. I will wear my hat. I really want to come with you. I have only seen pumpkins in vegetable shops and they're never with the vines. Please let me come,' Nooni persisted.

Ajja signaled for her to join him. Nooni hurriedly grabbed her hat and Ajja picked up his umbrella.

By the time the four of them reached the farm, the work was already in full swing. There were hundreds of pumpkins of different sizes and shapes lying in heaps. Ajja sat on a chair and started giving instructions about which batch to load on which pickup truck and which pumpkins to be kept separately to distribute to his friends.

After about half an hour, things were moving smoothly. Nooni started talking to her grandfather, 'Ajja, do you know the story of Somanayaka and the maidens that came down from the moon?'

Ajja smiled, 'You must have heard this story from your grandmother.'

'Is it true? Is that really how Somanahalli got its name? Do you think that there is a well somewhere under the ground — maybe even below the farm or our house?'

'Nooni, that is all hearsay. I only know what our ancestors have told me.'

'And what did they say? Tell me, Ajja! I'm dying to know.'

Ajja barked a few more orders and began his story, 'Long, long ago, there lived a handsome king named Somanayaka. He was brave, kind, courageous and very generous. His kingdom lay in the delta between the rivers Varada and Tungabhadra. There was a thick forest around the area and many wild animals lived there. Sometimes, they would enter villages and scare the people, destroy the crops and eat the cattle. After a number of such complaints and no improvement in the situation, the king decided to hunt these wild beasts himself. Two days later, he went hunting on his horse with his soldiers by his side. Soon, he had left his soldiers far behind and lost his way.

'While searching for a way back, Somanayaka came across a hut where an old man was dozing on the verandah. There was nobody else around. The king got off his horse and waited for the old man to wake up. After some time, the old man opened his eyes.

'Somanayaka gently questioned him, "You look a little unwell. Are you feeling all right?"

'The old man shook his head.

'"Isn't anyone here to take care of you?" the king asked.

'"This is my home and I am all alone. I have no family. Actually, I was planning to go to Kashi but I fell sick so I decided to stay back."

'"Kashi is very far. Why do you want to go there?"

'"It doesn't matter. I won't be able to go in my current state of health anyway."

'Somanayaka introduced himself, "I am King Somanayaka. Come with me. I will take you to my kingdom and make sure that you receive the best treatment."

'The old man was surprised by the king's generosity and nodded.

'In a few hours, one of the soldiers found Somanayaka and all of them came back to the king's palace. The royal physician treated the old man and the king ensured that he was given good food and plenty of rest. The old man recovered completely within a month and when he was fit to travel, the king called him to his chambers and said, "Here is some money. Take it and travel to Kashi. Use it to fulfill your desire."

'The old man laughed, "I don't think I need to go to Kashi now. Maybe I can do what I want right here."

'"Tell me, why did you want to go to Kashi?" Somanayaka was curious.

'"O King, I am an architect. I have great plans to build a stepwell—not an ordinary one, but a well with beautiful statues, ornate pillars and seven Shiva temples. I have spent years fine-tuning my architectural plans and drawings. Some said that the king of Kashi is large-hearted and that he may be generous enough to fund my stepwell. But now, I know that you are no less. Your devotion and your generosity to a stranger has touched my heart in more ways than I can say. Sire, if you can help me with my dream, I will be honoured."

'The old man opened his tattered bag and laid out the drawings in front of Somanayaka. The drawings were immaculate and the designs intricate.

'Somanayaka was impressed. "I would like to construct this in my kingdom but it will require a lot of money. Then I will have to tax my people and I'm not sure that I want to do that to them," he said sadly.

'"Please don't worry about that. I don't want you to start this work with diffidence. If you allow me, I can help you a little. My entire clan of sculptors is a hundred miles away in another kingdom but I can call them here. I also know how to search for hidden wealth below the earth. Do you remember the hut you found me in? Hundreds of thousands of gold coins are hidden below the earth there. I didn't share this information with you at the time because I didn't know you. But it's time now.

Let's unearth the enormous wealth and use it for the construction of the temples. Then you won't have to tax your people."

'The king was surprised at this disclosure. He ordered his soldiers to unearth the gold coins. True to the words of the old man, the king discovered the hidden treasure.

'Soon, hundreds of sculptors came from everywhere and the work began with great gusto. Slowly but steadily, the work continued.

'It took the workers four years to complete the stepwell but the temples were majestic and magical. Whoever saw the temples in their last stages of completion simply stood and soaked in their beauty. The water source at the bottom had water so sweet that it tasted like nectar.

'A few days later, the old man handed over the temples to Somanayaka and said, "My dear king, the project is complete and my dream is realized. There isn't a more beautiful well in the south of India. But if I may advise you like a father, listen to my words carefully. Water is a source of energy. If this source of water gets contaminated, then our entire effort will have failed and the temple will no longer remain the way it is. Please make sure that people wash their feet before they come into the temple and everyone must be allowed to take only one pot of water away. I request you to regulate this. Also, please close the stepwell once every fortnight. This one-day break will allow the water to maintain its level. Never make an exception to this rule. Follow my guidance and the monument will stay the way it is for a very, very long time."

'King Somanayaka promised to do so and proclaimed in his kingdom, "There exists a beautiful stepwell dedicated to Lord Shiva in our kingdom. People who would like to go there and perform puja can do so but on one condition—they have to wash their feet and cleanse themselves before entering the stepwell. The water will be used for no other purpose except for drinking. Everyone can carry away one pot of water and no more. These rules are to be strictly followed and there will be no exceptions. The temples will remain closed on full moon nights and nobody will be allowed inside."

'Somanayaka wanted to make his people comfortable so he ensured that there was another water body for them near the stepwell. People could bathe there, change their clothes and then enter the stepwell.

'The news spread like wildfire. People came from all over the kingdom to see the architectural masterpiece and pay their respects to Lord Shiva. The well remained open on all days except on full moon nights.

'Days passed and word spread even further. People started coming from far and wide and from different lands. A small tourist spot was set up near the stepwell and named Somanahalli.

'Despite the increase in the number of visitors, the well was kept clean and guards monitored the well and the activities during the day. Vigilant officers were hired to take care of the premises at night.

'Months later, the king was blessed with a baby boy. He was named Shashi Shekhara. Years passed and the prince grew into a young lad. Though he was smart, he was rather arrogant. One day, the king decided to go for a three-month pilgrimage with the queen to north India and handed over the reins of the kingdom to his son in his absence. The king told him, "My child, you are the future king. You must learn as much as you can from your own experiences and from observing others' lives. You should be humble, respect people who are older than you, understand your subjects and make all decisions keeping their welfare in mind. Only then can you succeed and become a great ruler."

'Prince Shashi Shekhara nodded but didn't really care for his father's words.

'The king warned him about the rules of the stepwell and instructed his son to follow them until his return. Shashi Shekhara happily agreed.

'Once the king left the kingdom, Shashi Shekhara and his friends became the lords of the land. They were young, with no wisdom and no authority figure to stop them.

'The prince's friends told him, "Your father is very old-fashioned and hates to experiment. Decades ago, an old architect dictated some rules to him and he is following them to this day. If something happens, you have enough wealth to create another stepwell. Water is meant for fun. It will be wonderful to bathe and swim in the stepwell. Why don't we do that the next full moon night? When your father comes back, you can show him that there's nothing special about that old fool's rules."

'Shashi Shekhara got carried away by his friends' words and recklessly went on a full moon night to swim in the well. The officers at the entrance stopped him but he arrogantly replied, "I am your ruler now and the land belongs to me. I can make the rules as easily as I can destroy them. Nobody can stop me."

'He pushed the officers aside and went inside with his friends. They swam and played there, drank the water, made fun of old people and came back to the palace.

'The next day, Shashi Shekhara made a new proclamation, "The stepwell will be used as a swimming pool for the prince and his friends. They can come any time they want. People can also take as much water as they want. There will no rationing, going forward."

'Within hours, people were carrying as much water as they wanted. Rich people carried more because they could bring a cart. In just two days, the water level started decreasing rapidly and soon, an epidemic occurred in the entire kingdom. People started getting high fever and vomited frequently. Their symptoms continued for days. No one realized that this was because the water had been contaminated. Nothing could cure the epidemic and people started dying.

'Shashi Shekhara was taken aback. He spent money freely to get the best medicines for his people and yet, he was unsuccessful at saving them. In four months, the kingdom was reduced to just a few thousand people. He lost his parents, the kingdom's crop and his soldiers.

'Shashi Shekhara now became worried about being conquered by a bigger army. He hated the stepwell. He thought it was the root cause of all evil and ordered his guards to fill it up with mud.

'In less than a year, Somanayaka's beautiful kingdom was conquered by his neighbours and all was lost.'

'Ajja, is this really true?' asked Nooni.

'I don't know but this is what I've heard from my elders. We stay in the same Somanahalli. When I was young, many people tried to locate the well but with no luck. Maybe it is all hearsay or maybe it occurred elsewhere. Maybe our ancestors made up this story because the name of our village is Somanahalli. Who knows? But one thing's for certain—never disobey your elders' words if they ask you to take something seriously. It comes from experience. And don't forget, Nooni. We should use our natural resources like water carefully.'

'Yes, Ajja, I know. I've always seen you take half a glass of water twice rather than a full glass of water and leaving some to waste. Ajji also doesn't allow me to have a shower. Usually, she gives me only one bucket of water,' Nooni added.

She recalled that there was no bucket in her apartment in Bangalore—she only had the option to shower. Despite that, her mother made sure that Nooni got exactly seven minutes to shower, otherwise the water would automatically turn cold instantly.

By this time, the pumpkin heaps on the trucks looked like yummy orange mountains. Nooni sat in the front seat of the pickup truck with her grandfather. It was much cooler than her father's car, or so she thought.

Within minutes, they were headed towards the nearest vegetable market.

Picnic at Varada River

After a few days of cycling everywhere, Nooni wanted to do something different. The days were getting hotter and so she decided that she wanted to swim. She requested her grandfather, 'Ajja, I want to swim in the Varada river. Now that I can cycle, I can go on my own. What do you think?'

'Nooni, it is not a good idea. The river is not a swimming pool. Don't become overconfident just because you know swimming and cycling. You are still a child and you must remember that you should be supervised in these sorts of places. I will take you to the river myself but let us plan this sensibly. Why don't we have a picnic tomorrow? Ajji, Savita and I will drive to the river in our pickup truck. We will bring raw vegetables and other ingredients so that we can cook on the banks of the river. You and your friends can come on your bicycles and once you reach the river, you can swim under Mahadeva's and my supervision. Then we will eat and come back home.'

Though Nooni did not like the idea of grown-ups accompanying her and her friends on a picnic, she was tempted by the thought of eating a home-cooked meal after a swim. She knew that Ajja rarely stopped her from doing anything. So he must have a good reason for not letting her go alone and she readily agreed.

When Ajji heard about their plan, she was very excited. She started packing the vegetables at night and also invited Sarasu Ajji to the picnic. The two women happily discussed the menu for the next day—chapatti, sabzi and bisi bele hulianna, a specialty of Karnataka. For dessert, they would take dry gulab jamuns. Savita also got busy collecting other items such as mats, vessels, wood, a stove, steel plates, brooms and plastic bags. She knew that Ajji would like to clean the picnic spot before leaving it.

The next morning, Ajja and his team left for the river at seven while the children met at seven-thirty and began their ten-kilometre trip to the river on their bicycles. This was the first time that Nooni was riding her cycle outside the village. Cycling on the uneven roads was not easy. However, Nooni carefully cycled at a moderate speed. Suddenly, Amit zoomed ahead. Then he took a U-turn and came back to join the rest. After some time, he showed off his cycling skills by lifting both his hands off the handlebar and reverse cycling immediately after that.

On the way, the children stopped for a few minutes to admire the countryside and the growing crops. Nooni desperately wanted to stay a little longer to find out the names of the crops and their lifecycle but she knew that that would delay them and then Ajja would get worried.

By the time they reached the banks of the river, the three women had settled into kitchen-related activities on an old mandap that had been built long ago. It was on the top of a stone hill and was clean and spacious. From there, the women could easily see the river. Ajja was the only man around and Nooni smiled as she saw him from a distance supervising their work.

As the children parked their cycles and walked closer to the water, Nooni noticed the absence of the smell of chlorine. Ajja held out a hand, signalling the children to stop where they were. First, he got into the water. Then he turned to Mahadeva and said, 'I shall check to see the point up to which the children can swim. They should start from here and keep away from the fast-moving water.'

'Ajja, are there any crocodiles here?' Nooni asked, recalling a movie that she had seen.

'No, this river does not have crocodiles but there may be some fish around. Listen now, children. Don't even try your diving skills here. There are stones at the bottom and you will end up getting hurt badly. Can you see that half-immersed stone there?' Ajja pointed out to a rock a short distance away. 'You can swim till there and rest on the stone. Then when you are comfortable, you can swim back. If you think you can't come back on your own, shout out to Mahadeva or me and we will come.'

Amit was disappointed. 'What's the point in swimming such a short distance? I want to cross the river and reach the other side!'

Ajja shook his head and refused his request.

Anand did not know swimming. He said, 'I will be happy just dipping my feet in the water.'

Medha knew how to swim but she was not

adventurous and was happy to simply splash around in the water.

Nooni knew swimming very well because of her previous lessons at the summer camps. She was excited—she wanted to know how it felt to swim in a river. Suddenly, she had a thought. She asked Ajja, 'How do I know the direction of the river?'

Ajja smiled, 'That's very easy. Pluck a small leaf, set it free in the river and just observe it. The direction it sails in is the direction of the river.'

Nooni didn't reply. She looked at Ajji and then ran towards her.

Ajja was taken aback at her abruptness.

When Nooni reached Ajji, she found her busy cutting vegetables. Slowly, Nooni whispered in her ear, 'Ajji, I want to use the toilet before I start swimming.'

Ajji laughed.

'You don't need a toilet for that. Go behind the bushes over there,' Savita said loudly and showed her the bushes that she was referring to.

Nooni was shocked. She looked at her grandmother and whined, 'Ajji, how can I do that? It's unhealthy and I have never done it in the bushes before.'

Ajji understood Nooni's problem. She said softly,

'My child, you are right. Unfortunately, there are no toilets in this area. If it is urgent, then you will have to do as Savita suggests. I will come with you and stand with my back towards you. This way I can cover you and nobody will see you.'

'No, Ajji, I can't do this,' Nooni refused.

'Then you may dirty the water when you can't control it anymore. So it's better to use the bushes,' Ajji persisted.

She pulled Nooni's hand and went with her behind the bushes.

After the bathroom business, Nooni slowly walked back to the water. Her friends were already playing around in the river. Since Nooni had worn a swimsuit underneath her clothes, she quickly pulled off her T-shirt and jeans and jumped into the water. It was cold but she got used to it within a few minutes and started enjoying herself. It was more fun than swimming in a pool. A pool restricted the area she could swim in and it was usually too crowded during the summer. People would inevitably bump into her but here it was blissful. She swam for some time, rested on the half-immersed stone and then swam again and splashed around with her friends till she was really tired.

'I wish I could do this every day,' she thought.

Soon, it was lunch time and she heard Ajji's voice saying, 'Children, get out of the water. Lunch is served!'

By then, everyone was hungry and they happily got out of the water. Ajji gave them all towels to wipe themselves dry.

While drying her hair, Nooni asked Ajja, 'Where does this river come from? And where does it go?'

'Every river has an origin. The Ganga comes from Gangotri and the Yamuna from Yamnotri. In the same way, Varada originates from a perennial water source in a village in the Sagar district of Karnataka. Small rivers merge into big rivers and big rivers join the sea.'

'Ajja, is the river always this wide?' Amit piped in.

'No, the Varada's width reduces in the summer but in the rainy season, she swells to three times her current size. But the water will not be clean then—it will be muddy and dirty with the high current. Nobody swims here at that time.'

'Why are you referring to river Varada as a "she"?'

'Because she is like a woman—she gives and gives and gives. Women are compassionate and they give their life for their family—just like your

Ajji does for our family and your mom does for yours,' said Ajja easily.

Ajji beamed at his words.

The group ate a simple meal at the mandap. The children were so hungry that they ate four times their normal ration.

Immediately after their meal, Amit, Medha, Anand and Nooni felt very sleepy.

Ajja saw their droopy eyes and said, 'Mahadeva, lay out the mats for the children to sleep. After their nap, we will leave and get back home before sunset.'

A few hours later, the adults drove back to the village and the children rode their cycles back to their respective houses.

That night, Nooni and her grandparents were alone for dinner. Ajji suggested, 'Gowri is out of station and it will be hard for Shankar Master to cook for Anand and himself. Let's call them over for dinner.'

Ajja agreed. He loved talking to Shankar Master and frequently called him over to his house. 'Let's call them,' Ajja said. 'Shankar Master is the only person in this village who can teach us about new things. He has travelled a lot and reads even more.

He also surfs the Internet every day. I am old now and prefer to learn from people like him. It makes me feel young too!'

Shankar Master came to the house an hour before dinner. At first, there was a discussion about the changes at the village school. Suddenly, Ajja remembered, 'Shankar, Nooni was asking me about the story of Somanayaka, Somanahalli and the stepwell. I have told her all I know. You are well-versed in history. Is there anything that you can tell us about the stepwell of Somanahalli?'

Shankar Master smiled shyly and said, 'No, sir. I am not as learned as you think, but yes, I love to read. When I was doing my Masters in history, I used to talk a lot to my professor and I am still in touch with him. When we were chatting the other day on Skype, this subject came up and what he told me was a real eye-opener.'

'What did he tell you?' Ajja asked inquisitively.

Ajji overheard the conversation from the kitchen and came out to hear what Shankar Master was going to say. Ajji had never had the opportunity to go to college but she was an avid learner and perpetually curious.

'He said that the delta between the Varada and Tungabhadra rivers was ruled by many small kings, who were individually known as Paleyagararu. They were subordinate kings to an emperor. While they were autonomous in their day-to-day activities, they were obliged to pay tax to the emperor and send their soldiers to join the emperor's army in case of a war. My professor believes that Somanayaka was one of these Paleyagararus. Historians have found many inscriptions from a thousand years ago where Somanayaka talks about his kingdom — the temples, ponds, mango groves and other places.'

'Can we read those old inscriptions too? Are they in the same Kannada that we use today?' asked Ajja.

'No, the script and the vocabulary are both different from today's Kannada. It needs expertise.'

'What does it say?' Ajji chimed in.

'The inscription says that Somanayaka, the son of Maranayaka, was a great warrior. He was brave, kind, courageous and very generous. His kingdom lay in the delta between the rivers Varada and Tungabhadra. There was a thick forest around the area and many wild animals lived there. Somanayaka used to hunt and protect his people and cattle. He was religious and built many temples to Lord Shiva, Lord Vishnu, Veerabhadra and others. He opened a university of higher learning, looked after its teachers and gave them land. He is believed to have constructed a large tank to help the farmers with irrigation and water problems and he also provided his subjects with drinking water in many areas of his kingdom.'

'Is there anything about a stepwell?' Nooni interrupted impatiently.

'There is an inscription that says that he built many stepwells, including one in Somanahalli, which was supposed to be magnificent. The inscription describes a beautiful water body and seven temples inside the stepwell. The thing is that the inscription was discovered around fifty miles away from Somanahalli. So we don't know if this is the real Somanahalli, or if it was another village that has changed its name over a period of time, or maybe it was a Somanahalli in another area. Who knows? But to our knowledge, that marvellous stepwell does not exist. There have been several excavations around this area before and none have even hinted at its existence.'

Nooni looked disappointed.

Ajji patted her head and said, 'Come, come. See what I've made for dessert—your favourite laddoos!'

It was enough to distract Nooni.

'Oh please, can I have three?' Nooni pleaded with her grandmother as she followed her to the kitchen.

The Cow's Delivery

When Ajji went to the cattle shed around ten the next morning, she hurriedly came back and told Savita, 'Call Taiawaa. I have a feeling that Kamadhenu is going to deliver today.'

Nooni was standing on the side and overheard the conversation. She asked, 'Ajji, how do you know that?'

'I have years of experience taking care of cattle. Earlier this morning, Kamadhenu did not drink water properly. She hasn't been able to sit comfortably either and her stomach is bulging. She is trying to tell me that the time to deliver her calf has come. I'm not going anywhere tomorrow or the day after. Kamadhenu needs me. Child, will you please go and inform Sarasu Ajji and my friends in the temple that I won't come until the calf is born?'

'Of course, Ajji. I will go in five minutes,' Nooni replied.

Then Ajji turned to Savita and instructed her, 'Soak a lot of rice in water, grate some coconuts and add jaggery. I'll bring some herbs from the garden and you can grind everything together. Then we'll put it in a big bowl and offer it to Kamadhenu.'

'Ajji, why are you feeding that to Kamadhenu?'

'It will help her prepare for the delivery.'

'But if she's about to give birth, we must take her to the animal hospital. You can't take good care of her at home.'

'Nooni,' Ajji explained patiently, 'our vet comes here only once a week. That's why I have called Taiawaa. She is trained to handle deliveries and is equivalent to a vet during these times.'

As Ajja passed by, Ajji called out to him, 'Please make sure that Kamadhenu does not go out to graze with the other cows today and arrange for some fresh green grass from the gomala. We will need the shed properly cleaned so that it is ready for the delivery. Later, I also want a big drum of water for cleaning up after the calf is born.'

Ajja nodded.

Meanwhile, Ajji hardly cooked anything for the

day—there was only roti and one vegetable curry. Her mind was on Kamadhenu.

Nooni also wanted to witness the delivery. After she came back from informing Ajji's friends at the temple, she asked her grandmother, 'Can I come inside the shed to watch and maybe help Taiawaa and you?'

'No, Nooni, this is not the time. You are too young and Kamadhenu may not like too many people around her. She is used to Taiawaa and me. You can sit outside with your grandfather and I will call you as soon as the calf comes out.'

'Okay, Ajji,' said Nooni. She knew her grandmother was worried. To distract her, she asked her another question, 'Ajji, how did you name the three cows?'

'Well, Ganga is the oldest. She is named after our sacred river. Without the river Ganga, India wouldn't have existed. Our ancient scriptures were written and civilization flourished on the banks of this river. Our cow Ganga has become old and doesn't give us milk anymore but she will stay with us until she dies because this is her home. Kamadhenu and Basanti are her daughters.'

'How did Kamadhenu get her name?' Nooni asked impatiently.

Ajji broke into a smile. 'Kamadhenu is the name of a divine cow who gives her owner whatever he asks for. She does the same thing for me—she gives our family plenty of milk and milk products like yogurt, butter, ghee, paneer and buttermilk.'

'And what about Basanti?'

Ajji laughed heartily. 'Basanti is not a traditional name for a cow at all. Thirty years ago, your grandfather saw a Hindi movie called *Sholay* in which the heroine was named Basanti, and since then he's always been crazy about that name. When you were born, he wanted to name you Basanti but your parents preferred Anoushka. So instead of you, we named the third cow Basanti.'

Nooni giggled.

'We also have two oxen—Ram and Lakshman. We bought them together from the market when they were young.'

After lunch, Ajja went to take a nap and Ajji went to the cowshed to check on Kamadhenu. Nooni sat in the verandah and started reading a book. Occasionally, she took a break to learn a few words from the dictionary. When Taiawaa—a dusky old lady wearing a green cotton sari and a pallu on her head—arrived, Ajji's face lit up and she asked her, 'Come, Taiawaa, have you eaten yet? If not, I'll bring you something to eat. Today is a big day for Kamadhenu.'

Taiawaa smiled and displayed her paan-stained teeth. 'Amma, I had lunch already. This is Kamadhenu's third delivery. Though she may be experienced by now, we still have to help her through the pain. I want to go and see her now.'

Taiawaa went inside the shed with Ajji. Nooni heard them talking to each other through the open door and she came running to the shed. Ajji heard her footsteps and closed the bamboo door. Still, Nooni could hear them faintly. 'I think she will take a few more hours, but not much longer than that. Just pat her and reassure her for some time. Then we will wait outside and monitor her regularly till it's time.'

After almost fifteen minutes, Ajji and Taiawaa came out.

'Ajji, why were you petting Kamadhenu?' Nooni accosted her as the door of the cowshed opened.

'Animals are like human beings, Nooni. When they are in agony, they also feel nice when someone stays with them and pats them, just like you ask for your mother when you are unwell. They may not be able to talk like us but they have the same feelings that we do.'

'Amma, will you give me betel leaf and areca nut? I enjoy eating paan,' said Taiawaa.

'I can give you plenty but don't spoil the shed by spitting all over it. Use the sink at the back and spit there,' Ajji told her firmly but affectionately.

'Amma, your house is the only one in the village that grows both areca nut and betel leaf. That's why I always ask you for it,' added Taiawaa.

Ajji was always neat and clean. Her saris were pearly white and she starched them every day. She combed her hair properly, made a bun and wore a flower. She hardly wore any ornaments but her broad smile was very attractive. Everything in her house was tidy and well-kept. She did not allow any footwear into the house. Nooni knew that Ajji was strict with everyone when it came to cleanliness.

Taiawaa and Ajji settled down on a bench near the cowshed and a few hours passed as they talked about several things and checked in on Kamadhenu at intervals.

Suddenly, there was a loud shriek. Ajji and Taiawaa rushed inside the cowshed. Nooni wanted to peep through the bamboo sticks at the door but then she remembered Ajji's instructions and changed her mind. She waited outside impatiently.

After some time, Ajji said loudly, 'Nooni, Kamadhenu has given birth to a baby girl. I will bring her outside so you can see her.'

Ajji came out with a small white calf with half-closed eyes. It was bigger than Nooni had thought it would be. She wanted to touch the calf but Ajji stopped her. 'Don't do that. Her mother has to lick her and love her first. Go wash your hands and feet and come inside the shed.'

Nooni ran to do her grandmother's bidding. When she came back, she could hear Taiawaa cleaning the cowshed with a broom. Quietly, Nooni went inside the shed and stood near Kamadhenu, who was licking the baby affectionately. The baby nuzzled her mother's neck and it almost looked as if she was smiling.

Varada Hill

There was a small hillock almost halfway between Somanahalli and the Varada river. It was called Varada Hill. Nooni had noticed it during the picnic to the river. She knew that every morning, two men gathered cattle from everyone's houses and directed them to the outskirts of the village. Then they took the cows to Varada Hill where there was plenty of grass for them. The cows usually grazed all day. The men carried their lunches and came back with the cattle in the evening. They returned the cows to their respective owners and sheds before going home for the day.

All the animals in Ajji's cowshed had a bath either in the morning or in the evening. Every animal had a bell of a different colour. Once the cows left the shed, it was cleaned thoroughly. The shed had a cement floor and it was washed so well that there were no flies and no smell. The water canal was also rinsed and fresh water was stored there again.

There was a storeroom containing dry grass and animal feed. Each cow had a small cement placeholder for their feed. Feeding was done in the mornings and in the evenings.

A few mornings later, Nooni woke up eager to visit the hill with her friends. She told Ajji and Ajja about her plan.

Ajja said, 'Take Mahadeva along with you. He will take you there safely. Go in the afternoon and come back by evening.'

Ajji called Mahadeva and gave him a bag of rice and a box of sugar. 'These are for the ants and squirrels,' she said.

Nooni wondered why her grandmother wanted to give rice and sugar to the little animals. She packed her backpack excitedly. After lunch, Ajja and Ajji said goodbye to her and retired to their room for a nap. Nooni's friends met her at the school ground and they began their hike.

The weather was warm but Medha didn't feel the heat. She said that she was used to it. Amit was happy that it was cooler than Delhi. Anand and Mahadeva were indifferent to the heat but Nooni wanted to protect her head so she grabbed a hat from her backpack.

They took a left turn at the main road and suddenly saw plenty of trees and bushes along the road.

Mahadeva saw a line of ants marching towards a hole in the ground. He took a handful of sugar from Ajji's box and sprinkled it in their way. He told the children, 'Please keep an eye out for the ants. Whenever you see them, let me know and I will give each of you a handful of sugar so you can give it to them.'

'Why, Mahadeva?'

'It is Ajji's idea. Later, I will also keep a handful of rice under some big trees. That's for the squirrels. Ajji says that when she built their house, many squirrels and ants that lived on her land were displaced from their home. Since then, she likes to feed ants, squirrels and birds. It is a very noble thought. I think she is a very kind-hearted person.'

Nooni found it amusing but agreed with her grandmother. They saw so many animals that the rice and sugar was over in no time.

Suddenly, Nooni saw a small, white cat-like animal that whisked past them and disappeared in a second. 'What's that?' she asked.

'That's a black-naped hare. They come out of hibernation this time of the year. They are shy and very fast.'

'Oh, we should have saved some rice for them too,' said Anand.

As the children walked further, they saw something yellow on the ground.

Nooni picked up a twig and touched it. It looked and felt like wax. 'What is this?' she asked.

'That is leftover wax from a hive. Nooni, be careful of honeybees. They can sting you badly.'

'But why would they sting me?' she asked innocently.

'If someone troubles you or throws stones at your house, you will get irritated, won't you? In the same way, they don't like it when anyone messes with their hive,' said Mahadeva.

'Nooni, if you stop every second, we won't be able to make it to Varada Hill. Let's move quickly,' said Medha, sounding a little annoyed.

Nooni nodded and the group started walking faster. Within a few minutes, they realized that the vegetation was thinning. Soon, there were no trees at all. There was a plain field with grass as tall as Nooni, with a small pond in the centre. A clear path was marked in the mud and the children quickly marched on it. To a distant spectator, only the children's heads bobbing up and down would have been visible as they made their way through the tall grass.

Within minutes, the group saw a small hillock with a big neem tree at the top. There were small steps leading up to the hill and the children quickly climbed to the top. From there, they could see their village and the Varada river, which was shining like silver in the bright sunshine. It was cool under the shade of the neem tree and the children settled down on some natural stones that worked as makeshift benches.

'Why is it called Varada Hill? It should be called one tree hill,' Nooni commented.

'There is a story behind how this hill was named,' said Medha. 'Seventy years ago, there lived a young boy called Varada. He was the son of a rich farmer and was an avid reader. While he was studying in a college in Dharwad, India was still colonized by the British. During that time,

Gandhi called the people of the nation to join the Quit India Movement. Varada wanted to join him but his parents opposed the idea. After a lot of discussion, he became convinced that the country was more important than his parents' wishes and joined the movement. He burnt all his silk apparel and switched to khadi clothing. He came every day to the hill to sit here and read. As he became more active in the movement, he started writing letters about it and sent them everywhere he could. He helped many people join the movement.

'The British soldiers frequently showed up in the village and searched for him. Sometimes, he would hide near the hill and sometimes, he would go away to the forest. Despite the danger, he continued helping the country until one fateful day when he was caught and thrown in jail. He died here due to lack of treatment after becoming ill with typhoid. His parents and the entire village mourned him but they remained proud of his contribution to the national movement. From that day on, people in the village called this spot Varada Hill. His parents donated their land on which the village high school stands today. The school is named after him too—Varada High School. Every year, we march from our school to this hill and hoist the national flag in his memory.'

Medha fell silent.

Amit added, 'There were many people in the north of our country such as Bhagat Singh and Chandra Shekhar Azad who also gave their lives for our freedom. In the Delhi cantonment, the gardens are named after the patriots and soldiers who died protecting our nation.'

Amit looked around and asked, 'Why aren't there any trees here? I can only see grass everywhere.'

'This is our village's gomala,' replied Mahadeva. 'Since the old days, every village has a gomala and a nagabana.'

'What's that?' asked Nooni. 'We don't have anything like that in Bangalore.' She felt a little conscious of the fact that her knowledge was limited compared to that of her friends.

'I haven't heard about it in Delhi either,' added Amit.

'A gomala is a piece of land that doesn't belong to an individual and isn't up for sale. It is village land where nothing except green grass is allowed to grow. Nobody can cut the grass or take it home. The land usually has a pond too. The grass is for the animals to graze and the water is free for them to drink.'

'So it's like a mid-day meal programme?' Nooni asked innocently.

Everyone laughed.

'This place reminds me of another story,' said Anand softly. 'In Sindh, in the Punjab of undivided India, there was a hillock just like this one. One day, an English officer was passing by the hill on his way to work. He brought his horse to a halt and asked a local man standing nearby, "What is the name of this hill?"

'"Mohenjodaro, the hill of the dead," the man replied.

'The officer was surprised.

'Later, someone told him that the reason for the name was because there were a lot of skeletons inside the ground in the area. The English officer ordered the excavation of the land and that's how we found the greatest civilization of them all—Mohenjodaro and Harappa.'

'Oh, what if there's a stepwell buried somewhere here too?' asked Nooni with enthusiasm. 'Or maybe we'll find something else here! Who knows? Just like Vikramaditya's throne, we may find Somanayaka's throne too!'

'What is that?' Mahadeva, Amit, Anand and Medha asked in unison.

Nooni began, 'Last year, I had gone with my parents to Ujjain. My dad was attending a conference there. So while he was busy during the day, Mom and I visited various monuments and she told me a lot of stories about them. She said that long, long ago, there lived a king called Vikramaditya. He was famous for his wisdom. After he died, his palace collapsed and over time, people forgot about it.

'After hundreds of years, a man was passing by the area when he saw a few young cowherds fighting amongst each other. The man stopped to watch them. One of the young boys intervened and said playfully, "Okay, stop fighting. I'll be the judge and solve your dispute. But a judge must sit in a proper place."

'There was a small hillock nearby and the boy found his way to the top. The other cowherds remained below. As the boy sat on the hilltop, he suddenly became authoritative and quickly resolved the issue. Then the boy came down from the hillock and became playful again. Within a few minutes, there was another dispute among the boys. This time, another boy said, "I will be the judge now."

'He went to the top of the hillock and passed the correct decision within minutes. The man saw all of this and wondered, "Maybe it's the place and not the person that's giving the right ruling."

'Soon, he went back to his village only to find a terrible argument going on in the panchayat. Since the man was known to be wise, the panchayat looked towards him for advice. The man suggested, "Come with me. Let's go to a hillock nearby. I will give the judgment there."

'When he made the right decision, everyone was happy and surprised. The man disclosed his observations to the crowd and the rumour began that if there was any dispute in the village, all one had to do was sit on the hillock.

'Word spread and reached the king of the land, who ordered careful unearthing of the hillock. After much digging, a beautiful throne was discovered. People said that it must be the throne of King Vikramaditya,' Nooni took a deep breath and ended her story.

'So, you see,' she added. 'You never know what lies beneath us. I wonder what's below this hill? I bet there's something unusual.'

'Nooni, don't think too much. It's getting late,' said Anand.

Almost as if on cue, the other children also got up, gathered their belongings and the group began to walk back home.

An Unusual Rain

The next few days after the trip to Varada Hill were very hot in Somanahalli. Ajja commented, 'This weather is really good for mangoes but such summer days are not going to last long. I'm sure it will rain soon. While the rain will settle the dust and cool the temperature down, it is not good news for the farmers.'

Ajji agreed, 'Yes, I think we should finish making papads before the rain gets here. A few of the women from the village are coming here today so that we can make the papads together. Once the sky is overcast, the papads won't get sunbaked properly and if they aren't dry enough, they will develop fungus in the winter.'

Ajja and Ajji continued their conversation on the weather but Nooni wasn't really listening. She was thinking about how her parents' conversations seemed to revolve only around how many patients Dad had, or how the bank was changing its systems and staff, or the best classes for her to attend. Her parents had deep discussions about their daughter's future school or college and how she could succeed in competitive exams.

Nooni sighed. It was a really different world out here in the village.

Within a few hours, Ajji and the women were rolling the papad dough in the spacious kitchen. Amit, Medha and Anand came over to play with Nooni but Ajji had other plans for them. She instructed the three of them to take the papads up to the terrace and place them on plastic sheets to allow the sun to bake them. Nooni and the other children ran up and down from the terrace to the ground floor with the papads. Amit and Medha stayed back on the terrace with a stick in their hands—ready to scare away the crows if they came to lift or disturb the wet papads.

When the women weren't looking, Amit, Medha and Nooni ate the wet papads. To Nooni's surprise, they tasted much better than the sun-dried version!

When Medha suggested they ask Ajji for some papad dough, Nooni happily agreed.

The children requested Ajji, 'Please give us some of the papad dough.'

Ajji was reluctant. 'Children, if we bake the papads and store them properly, they will last us for at least a year. In the rainy and winter season, you can eat fried papads which will taste excellent with your food.'

But Nooni insisted, 'In any case, you will fry the papad for us later. Ajji, if you give us the dough now, we won't ask you for more.'

Ajji smiled sweetly and gave them a big bowl of dough to eat.

Nooni fell in love with the papad dough—it was more delicious than both the wet and dried papads. She wanted more but Ajji refused.

'Too much of anything is bad,' she said. 'You will stop enjoying it as much if you eat a lot of it.'

The children nodded and ran away to play.

By afternoon, dark clouds had gathered in the sky. Immediately, Ajji turned to the women and said, 'Stop making the papads. Today isn't the day.'

She told Anand and Nooni, 'Once it starts drizzling, go to the terrace and cover the papads with a plastic sheet. If the rain gets worse, then bring the papads inside and spread them on the balcony.'

Less than five minutes later, it started drizzling. Nooni and Anand ran to cover the papads. But before they were barely halfway through, hail started pouring down.

Ajji shouted out to them from the kitchen below, 'Bring the papads inside. The hailstorm will destroy them.'

By the time the children started bringing the papads to safety, half were lost in the rain and the heavy wind. The hailstorm was so strong that Ajji eventually stopped them. 'Leave the papads, children. Stay inside the building. I don't want you to get hit by the hailstones. The stones are as big as lemons and they will hit you hard. We can always make more papads later.'

Amit, Medha, Anand and Nooni left the papads where they were and came inside and stood in the balcony that was attached to the terrace. They could still see the rain and feel the gushing wind. The leaves of the coconut trees looked like they were dancing vigorously and the garden in front of the house looked like a pond filled with rainwater.

Nooni was fascinated—she had never seen this kind of storm in Bangalore. She looked up at the scary, thunderous sky. It was dark even though it was just early evening. Soon, the terrace was covered with ice balls. Nooni was tempted to go out and grab some of them.

Suddenly, Ajji called out to them, 'Children, come down for some bondas and warm milk.'

'Ajji's food factory is always busy,' Nooni thought. 'She loves cooking and experimenting. She makes varieties of pickles, chutneys and salads and likes to feed people.'

When the children came down the stairs, they saw Ajji giving Mahadeva instructions, 'Close the doors of the cattle shed after checking for leaks and taking care of them. The poor animals . . . they can't even share their difficulties with us.'

Ajja, on the other hand, was sitting with two men in the living room. Nooni overheard them talking. 'It doesn't rain for more than a half an hour at a time during this season. But this time, the wind speed and hailstorm has taken me by surprise. I don't think I've ever seen it rain for two continuous hours during the summer season. This is so unusual,' one of the men commented.

'You're right,' Ajja agreed. 'This rain will destroy the mango crop and the vegetables too.'

The rain finally stopped after four long hours and everyone left for their homes. Though there were no leaks, Nooni could hear the water flowing around the house. She wondered how the Varada river must look. For a minute, she thought about grabbing her bicycle and biking to the river, but it was already dark and the roads were filled with water. She knew that her grandparents would not let her go. So she went to her grandfather. 'Ajja, don't you think that we should go and see the river right now? I have never seen what a river looks like after a heavy storm but I've heard that it's amazing.'

'If you really want to see the river, you and your friends can go with Mahadeva,' said Ajja. 'Tomorrow, there will be less water on the road and Mahadeva can drive you all in our pickup truck. If you want to get down at the river and walk in the mud, I'll tell him to guide all of you carefully.'

Ajji, however, was not too excited about the plan. She asked Nooni, 'What do you think you are going to see there? The river has only water and I don't want you to get stuck in the mud.

Nooni, when it rains, all the water comes on to the roads since there is no proper drainage system in our village. Also, the roads are not tarred and the earth absorbs the rain-water, and you may end up getting stuck in the mud and it can become very hard for you to even move.'

But Nooni did not listen to Ajji's warnings and made up her mind to go to the river anyway.

Is It a Stepwell?

The next day, the weather was cool but dark clouds lingered in the sky. Nooni told her grandparents, 'I am getting bored at home. I've asked Medha, Amit and Anand to join me. We are all going to see the Varada river. Ajji, please pack lunch for us — I will help you. We are going to hike today since the roads are not good for cycling after the rain. After our walk, we will go to the farm to play and I will come back in the evening.'

Ajji was not happy about this development. She said, 'Why do you have to go to the river? It may not be the best thing to do right now and it can be dangerous. I know that Mahadeva is with you but still, can't you sit and read or call your friends home and play here? Why do you always like to go here and there?'

But Ajja always encouraged Nooni to explore the outdoors. He said to his wife, 'Let her go out. She doesn't have this freedom in Bangalore. You know children have much so more energy than us! Pack some samosas, sandwiches and biscuits for the kids. Nooni, don't forget to fill all your water bottles. Many people will come to see the river today. It will be beautiful but you must not swim or get into the water. You can stand at the mandap to get a good view of the river. I will tell Mahadeva to make sure that you follow my instructions.'

Nooni went to the room to get her backpack. She checked her emergency kit—it had her cell phone, a torch, a folding stick, binoculars, a matchbox, a candle, a hat, an umbrella, a notepad and a pen, a small towel, wet wipes and a small first-aid kit given by her father. She always carried the kit whenever she had an outdoor activity planned. Sometimes, her friends made fun of her but she didn't care. She knew it was important to carry it.

Ajji told Mahadeva, 'You must be careful and take care of the kids. I am going to the temple for a puja today and will come back only in the evening. Bring the children home whenever they get bored or tired. Here, take this lunch basket. It is for all of you.'

'I am also going to the farm to take stock of the havoc created by the rain and wind. It will take time to clean and get things in order. I will be back in the evening,' Ajja added.

Ajji warned Mahadeva, 'Nooni is adventurous and wants to explore everything. She doesn't know the dangers of our terrain. You'd better take care of her. If she gets hurt, I will hold you responsible.'

Soon, Nooni and Mahadeva left the house to meet Amit, Medha and Anand. Nooni didn't understand Ajji's concern. Why was Ajji getting so worried?

By the time Mahadeva and Nooni reached the meeting point, the other children were already waiting for them. Amit was holding a catapult while Medha was carrying a backpack with paper and coloured pencils. She loved sketching and painting. Anand carried a few small mats and a book in his backpack.

'So where are we going today?' asked Medha.

'We are going to the riverbed,' replied Mahadeva. 'The road from the village to the riverbed is bad and we can get stuck on the way. So let's go through the forest. It will be a long interesting walk. I'm sure we will find a lot of mangoes, local berries like amla and plenty of jamun on the ground. They are safe to eat. I bet we will see deer too! Here, seeing a deer is almost as common as seeing a dog in the village streets.'

Nooni's daring spirit burst forth and she said excitedly, 'Let's do that! It will be an adventure!'

Medha said, 'Yes, I agree. On the way, I can stop to draw pictures of the deer, the trees and the forest.'

'And I can use my catapult. That way, I will get the unspoiled mangoes hanging on the trees. You all can take whatever you find on the ground. The trees are mine,' declared Amit.

Anand said, 'Anything is fine with me.'

'Come on then,' said Mahadeva and took the lead. He walked in front of the group with Nooni second and the others right behind her.

Though Nooni had gone on some adventures and hikes before, this was a little different. The forest itself wasn't very thick and there were many native trees, bushes and local mango trees, which were different from the usual hybrid variety. A few mangoes were lying on the ground and Mahadeva picked up one. 'This is a forest mango,' he said.

'How do you know?' asked Nooni.

'Forest mangoes are the fruits of the native mango trees here. Nobody plants or waters or grafts them. There is no manure or a gardener to look after them either. They are small in size and have big seeds and a sour taste. The birds and the monkeys in the forest usually eat these mangoes.'

Nooni picked up another mango from the ground, wiped it with a wet wipe and took a bite. It was extremely sour. Almost instantly, she remembered her father's advice, 'Don't eat any fruits or vegetables without washing them first.' She consoled herself by thinking that the heavy rain must have washed the mango.

They walked a little further and Mahadeva saw a plant with tiny, delicate pinkish flowers in their path. Before he could warn Nooni, she stepped on it. Suddenly, the leaves of the plant shrank and folded inward. She was surprised. She touched the plant curiously and the same thing happened again. 'What is this?' she asked.

'This plant is called the shy princess of the forest,' said Medha, who was right behind her.

'I have seen many such plants in school,' added Anand.

'The biological name for the plant is *Mimosa pudica*,' said Amit. 'My botany teacher said so. But in English it is popularly known as touch-me-not.'

'We call it *muttala muruki* in Kannada,' said Mahadeva. 'It means don't touch me.'

'Will they remain like this forever?' Nooni was curious.

'No, the leaves will open again after some time.'

Nooni found its pink flowers so attractive that she touched it again but because of her haste, a thorn pricked her. 'Nooni!' Mahadeva almost shouted. 'Don't touch any plants in the forest without knowing what they are. Most plants know how to protect themselves. If you touch some plants, you may feel itchy afterwards while other plants may ooze a sticky, white gum on to your hand. Be careful.'

Nooni nodded and the group continued walking.

After a distance, Nooni stopped and sniffed. There was a beautiful aroma in the air. She asked, 'What is this fragrance? I have never smelled it before.'

Medha giggled. They were passing under a bakula tree. 'Nooni,' she said, pointing to the tree. 'This is a bakula tree and its flowers are considered divine. The flower isn't very attractive but the fragrance is to die for. Even its dried flowers give the same smell. If you go to Ajji's cupboard, you will see a string of dried bakula flowers in there. All the women in the village keep bakula flowers in their saris because it helps ward off insects.'

Nooni felt humbled—she knew very little compared to Medha and Anand when it came to nature and its mysteries.

The children continued on their way. The terrain was definitely better than taking the main road. Though there was a little mud, there were enough stones for them to jump on and walk on.

'Look at that!' exclaimed Mahadeva. 'Sshhhh! Don't talk.'

The children saw two birds chirping away. A minute later, they were sharing the same guava.

Nooni asked ever-so-softly, 'What are those?'

But she wasn't quiet enough. Her whisper was loud and the birds flew away.

'They are myna birds. Haven't you read the story about the myna birds?' asked Anand.

'No,' said Nooni, suddenly angry that her friends seemed to know so much more about these birds.

'Myna birds are also known as lover birds. If one dies, the other one also dies. They are said to mate for life. And if you see a myna bird in the morning, people say that the day will be lucky for you.'

After that, no one spoke for a long time. There were just the sounds of the forest along with the sound of quiet footsteps.

'Look at that!' whispered Mahadeva and pointed to a big bird sitting all alone on top of a tree.

'That is a ratnapakshi,' said Amit.

'How do you know?'

'I've seen them in my backyard in Delhi. We live in the cantonment area where there are a lot of trees and birds. My mother says that if you see a ratnapakshi, you will definitely eat some dessert that day.'

Suddenly, the children stumbled on to a group of deer, who vanished the moment they heard them.

Nooni was very sad. 'I wish I could have seen them properly.'

'Don't worry, Nooni. You will see a lot of them. This is not the end of our journey. Deer are very sensitive animals and they run very fast. If you move quietly, you will eventually see them. There is a variety of deer here in this forest—some are dotted and some have beautiful antlers. And they are vegetarian,' said Anand kindly.

'Do the deer come into village?'

'Rarely. But I have seen them in our school during summer. They usually come to eat the vegetables from the kitchen garden in school,' said Anand.

'Does the school management get upset when they eat your vegetables?' asked Nooni.

'No, nobody stops them. My grandfather says that the land belongs to the deer too. So we should let them eat whatever they want. A few students have built a small pond for the deer to drink clean water. In fact, we have also dug a small pit and put salt in it.'

'Why would you do that?'

'Deer love salt so they come to lick the salty mud,' Anand replied.

As they walked further, Nooni noticed a strangely beautiful green creeper ahead of them. Mahadeva stopped near it and showed the group the chiguru, or the front portion of the vine. He cut it with a knife and offered a little bit of it to all the children.

Hesitantly, Nooni bit into it and exclaimed, 'Oh! It is sour but very yummy! What is it called?'

Everyone was blank.

'Maybe this is a forest creeper without a name,' said Medha.

'I have never seen it anywhere,' added Amit.

Anand asked, 'I have never noticed this creeper even though I have come to the forest many times. Is it a special plant?'

'Yes, it is special,' explained Mahadeva. 'This is the creeper that gives us the shikakai fruit.'

'Shikakai?' asked Amit and Nooni in unison.

'Yes, when you dry and powder shikakai, it can be used as a shampoo. Even Ajji uses shikakai powder to wash her hair. In the olden days, you didn't get shampoos in the market. So this was used as a natural shampoo since it is excellent for the hair. Sometimes, people use the fruit to make soaps too.'

Nooni said, 'Yes, Ajji has a box of shikakai powder in the bathroom. She washed my hair with it a few days ago. It made my hair really soft and nice-smelling. Even Indore Ajji uses an orange-coloured bar of shikakai soap to wash her hair. But my mother always uses shampoo and conditioner—just like me. I didn't know that I could wash my hair with a powder that came from a fruit. Isn't that just genius?'

'What's so great about this creeper?' asked Anand, interrupting Nooni.

'Pregnant deer love to eat chiguru because it contains natural iron and many vitamins, which are needed for their unborn babies,' answered Mahadeva.

'Hmm, animals don't talk but they are very intelligent, aren't they? Can we eat some more chiguru?' asked Nooni.

'No, let's not. This is meant for the deer and we are in their home, after all. The creeper grows very slowly and I think we should leave the rest for the pregnant deer.'

'Well, then can I eat the fruit? Where can I get more of it?'

'Fruits grow on the creeper every alternate year. People collect the fruits once they fall to the ground. Then they make a powder and use it.'

Nooni looked at Mahadeva with admiration—he was a walking encyclopaedia!

'Do you all want to walk more or do you want to rest for some time?' asked Mahadeva.

'Let's walk a little further and find a better spot with some shade. You must have come this way many times, Mahadeva. Can you find a nice place for us to rest?' asked Anand.

'Yes, there are many paths through the forest, but fewer people travel this route,' he said, 'there is a soap nut tree ahead with plenty of shade. Let's go and sit down there.'

'What is a soap nut tree?' asked Nooni. She seemed to have an unending list of questions and tremendous energy.

But by then, Amit, Medha and Anand were too tired to reply.

Mahadeva said affectionately, 'It is a local tree called antalkai. If you soak the sticky fruits of this tree in warm water, then the water can be used as a mild detergent or shower gel. A lot of women wash their silk fabrics with it because the solution does not discolour the garment and gives a nice sheen to the silk.'

'Is it like Genteel?' asked Nooni.

'I don't know what Genteel means, but the solution is gentle for sure!'

Less than ten steps ahead, Nooni encountered what looked like a betel leaf plant. 'Who planted this?'

'Nobody plants anything in the forest. Sometimes,

the birds or the wind carry seeds and other times, it is the rain or the water on the ground. Even animals like monkeys happily eat fruits and then drop the seeds here and there,' said Mahadeva.

'But this is paan, isn't it? Can I eat it?'

'We can't eat paan directly like this, silly! And this is not paan. I know that it looks like it but it is the leaf of the black pepper plant. When chilies did not exist in our country, black pepper was used as the main spice in cooking,' said Anand.

'What do you mean we didn't have chilies in our country?' Nooni was aghast at the thought. 'Chili is used in North and South Indian food!'

'I think you should start reading a lot more about these things, Nooni. You will then learn more about the history of the chili and who finally brought it to India. Guava, papaya, potato, onion, garlic, custard apple, apple . . . the lessons of history to be learned from these fruits are endless,' said Anand.

By then, the group had reached the soap nut tree and they all sat down to relax. It was a little after noon.

Nooni was looking everywhere curiously. She saw a large mushroom on the ground and was thrilled. 'Hey! I have never seen such a large

mushroom in the vegetables shops in Bangalore. Can we cut it and take it home for Ajji to cook? I love mushrooms.'

Medha went to the mushroom and examined it closely. 'Nooni, this is not an edible mushroom. Not all mushrooms can be eaten. Some are poisonous! Be careful and don't eat anything without checking with us first.'

But Nooni wanted to see more of the forest. It was as if a new world had opened up to her. As everyone settled down, Mahadeva started distributing water and fruits but Nooni didn't want to eat what Ajji had given them. She saw a shrub with wild berries at a short distance and asked, 'Can I pick those berries?'

'Oh, you will have to walk on that mud, Nooni. You'd better be careful,' warned Mahadeva, as he also sat down to eat and drink.

Nooni started walking on the mud path towards the shrub. Just as she was about to reach the shrub, she panicked—her shoes seemed to be stuck! She pulled with all her might but couldn't move. A few seconds later, she felt herself sink and the mud went up to her ankles. The more she tried to get free, the more she sank.

Finally, she shouted, 'Medha! Mahadeva! Please help me! I am sinking!'

Everyone came running to her. Mahadeva stopped everyone a few feet away, 'Don't go there. If you also start sinking, then I can't pull everyone out by myself. Listen to me—I will grab Nooni's hand and pull her out while you hold me and pull me back.'

With a lot of effort, Mahadeva pulled Nooni out, but her boots remained stuck. While Mahadeva was catching his breath, Nooni stared down at the mud—it kept falling down even though she was no longer there. She didn't understand why that was happening!

Abruptly, she said, 'Wait a minute! There's something else there, which is why the mud won't stop falling down. Why don't we see what's inside?'

'Come on, Nooni! Are you crazy?' said Medha.

'Please, Medha, let's see what's down there!'

'It's probably just a pit,' said Anand. 'There are many pits in the forest and if we keep stopping to check them out, we will never reach the river!'

But Nooni wasn't listening to them anymore. She suddenly thought of her boots. 'I want my boots back! How can I walk without them?'

'But Nooni, they are very dirty and I don't want to go there again!' Mahadeva sounded a little annoyed.

Nooni brushed past him and walked barefoot towards her boots. She stopped a little distance away when she saw that they were stuck under a rock. 'Will you help me move this rock so that I can grab my boots?' she requested Mahadeva, knowing that he was the strongest of them all.

'Nooni, I think the rock is too big for me and I don't want to get close to the falling mud.'

'Mahadeva, just look here. The mud is slipping inside the hole so quickly now. If we wait for much longer, my boots will also fall inside,' Nooni insisted.

Nooni lay on her tummy and grabbed her boots. Her clothes became muddy but she didn't care. She just wanted her boots back. Mahadeva caught hold of her legs and shouted loudly, 'Pull, Nooni, pull! We are holding you!' The three other children also joined Mahadeva and kept a firm hold on Nooni as she tried to pull her boots out from under the rock.

'Har har Mahadeva!' yelled Nooni.

Amit said, 'Dum laga ke haisha!'

The rock moved slowly and Nooni managed to get a hold of her boots. Mahadeva and the children pulled her back as she watched the rock begin to incline. In less than a minute, it fell down into the pit along with the slimy mud.

Nooni stood where she was, motionless.

Mahadeva and the others started dusting their hands.

'Let's get out of here,' said Medha.

'No, please, let's not go anywhere!' exclaimed Nooni. She took her torch out of the backpack and switched it on. 'There is something below the ground and it isn't a pit. I just know it. I'm going to go and check.'

'Nooni, I know that you listen to plenty of stories from Ajji. She is a wonderful storyteller and the whole village loves listening to her. But that doesn't mean that there is a palace of some princess below this stone!' said Medha.

'This has nothing to do with Ajji!' Nooni shone her torch at the pit from a distance. 'I think I can see a path. I'm going in!'

'Are you mad? There may be snakes down there. I'm scared!' said Medha.

'Who knows where the pit ends? Who will pull us out if we get stuck?' asked Amit.

'This could lead to anything! I don't want to get in trouble,' exclaimed Anand.

Once Nooni decided to do something, nothing could stop her. She looked at Mahadeva pleadingly. 'If you are ready to help me, I will go inside. If I get stuck, Medha, Amit and Anand can use my cell phone to call for help. And if there's no network here, they can run back to the village and inform everyone. Mahadeva, I would like you to come with me but if you don't want to, it's okay. Then I will go by myself and you can help me climb out later.'

Mahadeva could see the determination in her eyes. She may not know much about birds, animals and forests but she was adventurous, loved experimenting with new things and exploring the unknown. 'The worst that can happen is that we will get stuck in the pit,' he thought.

He smiled at Nooni. 'I will help you but let's do this sensibly.'

He looked around and saw a long wooden branch. He used the branch to push a big stone inside the pit. The stone fell and hit the bottom with a thud.

A little more mud fell inside. Mahadeva took two more long branches and slowly descended into the pit. He figured that the branches may help them find their way around or climb out later. Nooni followed him confidently with her backpack behind her. Finally, they were standing together on what seemed to feel like a step in a staircase.

There was a cave-like structure with a small opening ahead of them. Only tiny Nooni would be able to get in. She removed her backpack and bravely squeezed herself into the opening as Mahadeva watched her. 'Be careful, Nooni. We don't know what's inside. Do you have another torch? What about a matchbox?'

Nooni remembered the matchbox and cell phone inside her backpack. She said quietly, 'I can't turn around now so you will have to help me. Take the matchbox out of my bag and light a match or you can use my torch. I also have a three-fold stick. Pass it to me. I can use it to poke a few holes here and there. Maybe the mud will move a little bit so there's some space for you as well.'

Mahadeva handed Nooni the stick and within a short while of poking it around, she was able to make space for Mahadeva to get in. They lit

a matchstick and saw a black pillar on the side. Then they looked at it closely using the torch. Though the pillar was only exposed partially, it was clear that it was decorated with beautiful designs. The rest of the pillar was covered with mud, sand and stones.

They tried to explore some more but couldn't make their way further.

Finally, Nooni said, 'We can't do this by ourselves, Mahadeva. Let's widen the hole on the top so Amit, Anand and Medha can also get in.'

Slowly, Nooni started climbing the pit. Amit, Medha and Anand were silently sitting under a tree and waiting. They looked worried and scared. When they saw Nooni's cheerful face, with her head full of mud, they realized that she was safe. They rushed to give her a hand and pulled her out. Mahadeva was right behind her.

Nooni said happily, 'We saw a beautifully carved pillar and I bet there are more of them.'

'Really? I want to see it too!' added Amit.

'But we can't explore further without the right instruments. What should we do?' asked Mahadeva.

'Tell me, how far are we from the farm?' asked Nooni.

'Not very far. It's on the other side of the rivulet,' said Mahadeva. 'I can show you a shortcut to get there.'

'First, we need to clean ourselves and remove the mud. Once we reach the farm, I can take you to the extra room where Ajja keeps farming equipment like shovels, picks, metal baskets, brooms and ropes. Let's bring some of it here. We won't tell Ajja or Ajji what we're doing right now or else they will definitely stop us. I will tell my grandparents about this in the evening. So, do you all agree with me? Shall we do this on our own?'

Everyone looked at each other. They didn't know what to say.

Nooni stepped up to be their leader and said firmly, 'Listen to me now. Don't be scared. Nothing will happen to us. Come, let's have an adventure!'

The children decided to take the shortcut and reached the rivulet. The water came up to their knees because of the rain! They all took a dip in the water and cleaned themselves up. Then they crossed the rivulet and reached the farm. Nooni was right—there was plenty of farming equipment available. They quickly picked up whatever they needed and went back to the pit.

It was almost 2 p.m. and the sun was shining brightly in the sky. Nooni knew that her grandparents were busy for the day and that nobody would notice her long absence.

Mahadeva suggested, 'If we all work together, this may take only two or three hours.'

He took the pick and started removing the mud near the top of the pit. Nooni, Medha, Anand and Amit gathered the mud and started placing it on the side. Mahadeva was fast and within half an hour, there was a bigger hole on the top. Now, all of them could go in. When they went inside the pit, they saw another half-buried pillar.

Mahadeva said, 'I will collect the rubble and all of you can spread out. Help me throw the rubble outside the pit.'

Mahadeva got in first, followed by Nooni, Amit, Medha and Anand. Nooni lit a candle and put it on a stone. In the dim light, Mahadeva collected the rubble with a shovel, put it in a basket and passed the basket to Nooni. She passed it to Amit, who passed it to Medha and then Anand took it and threw it outside on the side of the pit. They kept cleaning out the rubble for almost two hours. Finally, the children uncovered three steps.

As soon as it started getting dark, all of them came out of the pit drenched in mud and dust. 'I can't go home like this,' Medha whined. 'My mother will ask me a lot of questions.'

'Don't worry, Medha. Let's go to the rivulet and clean up. By the time we reach home, our clothes will be dry,' said Nooni.

'A good wind will dry the clothes even faster,' commented Anand.

They rushed to the rivulet and cleaned up quickly.

On their walk back to the village, Nooni asked her friends, 'Can we go there tomorrow also and clean up?'

'Why do you want to do that?' questioned Amit.

'The five of us can't take on such a big task by ourselves,' added Anand.

'We did it today because you were insistent. What do we get by doing this?' asked Medha.

'I've heard from Ajji that there was a stepwell near our village. Then I heard a slightly different version from Ajja and Anand's father. Who knows? Maybe this is the same stepwell that everyone is talking about! If we unearth it, wouldn't it be awesome?'

'I don't know whether there is a stepwell here

or not. But either way, we are children and can't handle such a big project on our own. We have to tell the grown-ups,' said Anand.

'I agree,' said Mahadeva. 'I know I can work hard but even I think this structure is too big for one person to work on.'

'And what if we find poisonous snakes between the rocks as we work? What will we do then?' asked Medha.

'Can we get a bulldozer and unearth it?' suggested Amit, having seen plenty of bulldozers in the cantonment.

'There is hardly any place to walk, so you can forget about getting a bulldozer here,' laughed Mahadeva.

Nooni said, 'In that case, don't mention this to anyone in your homes. First, I will talk to Ajja and tell him about what we have seen. I have faith in him and I'm sure he won't refuse my request without a very good reason.'

Finally, they all reached home. Their families thought that they had only gone to the river. So they didn't worry much about their semi-wet clothes.

Nooni had a bath and changed her clothes. When Ajji went for her evening prayers to the other room, Nooni went and sat next to Ajja. He had had a long, tiring day cleaning the farm and was sitting on a rocking chair, trying to relax.

When he saw her, he said, 'Oh, Nooni, all our vegetables have been washed away and a few banana trees have fallen along with the tender coconuts because of the heavy wind. The mangoes are in the most terrible state—only a few of them are left. But there are plenty of raw ones. Your Ajji can make mango pickle for the entire village for several years,' laughed Ajja loudly, despite the ugly situation on the farm.

'What about the jasmine and champak trees in Ajji's garden?' Nooni asked.

'Well, surprisingly, they have survived. It's strange how the smallest of things can survive these calamities.'

'Ajja, I want to talk to you about something. I am sure you won't get upset with me.' Nooni took a deep breath and told Ajja about everything that had happened that day.

Ajja was surprised. 'Nooni, I think all of you have done something really commendable. Who else knows about this?'

'Just Mahadeva and my friends. We haven't told anyone else except you.'

'Keep it that way. I will call our panchayat head, Hanumegowda, and tell him about what you all have found. I will also inform Shankar Master. This is such good news.' He was excited.

Ajji had finished her prayers by then and overheard Ajja as she was passing by. 'What's happening? Why are you sending messages to Hanumegowda and Shankar Master at this time of the evening? Is it something urgent?'

'Yes, I think it is. Your granddaughter has found some temple ruins or maybe even a stepwell! I always thought that the stepwell incident was just a story. Now I'm beginning to wonder.'

Ajji was even more ecstatic than Ajja. 'I knew it! I knew that the stepwell would be found one day!' In her excitement, Ajji forgot to light the evening lamp in the puja room.

In a short while, Shankar Master and Hanumegowda joined them. Anand walked in behind his father. Mahadeva was already there helping Ajji with a few odd jobs.

All of them sat in the verandah.

Hanumegowda, who was in his late thirties, was an energetic person. Though he was educated, he had not looked for a job in the city. Instead, he started a greenhouse in Somanahalli and grew gerberas and gladiolas of different colours and sent them to Bangalore. He also looked after his father's fields. He had good business sense and was instrumental in ensuring that a bus from Haveri came to the village three times a day. Toilets were built in all houses in the village under his leadership. Ajja held him in high regard.

'Now, Nooni,' Ajja said. 'Tell us exactly what happened today.'

Nooni repeated the entire story. Mahadeva and Anand listened to her and added to the story every now and then.

After Nooni stopped talking, Shankar Master said, 'If it is really a ruin, then we have to inform the Archaeology Department about the discovery. They will send people to come and check the ruins, but the whole process will take time.'

'This is our village and the ruins belong to our land. We can't keep waiting for someone to come from the Archaeology Department and guide us. Those people will take their own sweet time. We should at least start the process,' said Hanumegowda with enthusiasm.

'That is true. However, it is our duty to inform

them. We can always start the work on the outside, but we must be careful not to destroy or spoil anything inside. It is an offence to do so.'

'When word gets around about our project, some people will think that money is hidden in the ruins,' said Hanumegowda, trying to analyze all aspects of the situation. 'Some might even come to dig the ground and in the process of trying to find the money, they will destroy the ruins. There are four hundred houses in our village. Let's talk to as many people as we can and choose a few strong and good men for security. We will tell them that there may or may not be money in this project, but that this place could be of great historical significance. It will belong to our village and we should be proud of it. In the unlikely event that we find any wealth at all, we will give it to the government in accordance with our current law.'

Suddenly, Hanumegowda swung into action and his tone changed. 'Shankar Master, you will be in charge of this project until the archaeologists come. And we will arrange for twenty-four-hour security with more people guarding the place at night.'

Ajji interrupted, 'Do you think that it is really a stepwell?'

'No one can say for sure at this point,' replied Shankar Master. 'These children may think that they have seen steps, but it may not be so at all! It could just be rubble or flat pieces of stone. Let's not jump to any conclusions before we know more.'

'When should we start the work?' inquired Ajja.

'We will start tomorrow,' said Hanumegowda. 'Shankar Master, can you find out which Archaeology Department we should contact and who our contact person will be? I will call up and talk directly to him or her.'

'If it comes under Bangalore's jurisdiction, then I can tell my son to find out more,' Ajja said.

'I'll have to google and see what I can find out. I'll go check the Internet,' said Shankar Master, and stood up.

'If the Internet is not working, Shanker Master, then call me. I will come and drop you at the cyber café at the taluka. It will definitely work there. Let's move fast,' said Hanumegowda and left in a hurry.

After everyone left, nobody wanted to eat dinner. They were still too excited.

Ajja called Shekhar. 'Son, do you know anyone in the Archaeology Department in Bangalore?'

'Appa, what a strange question! I am not a history student nor am I active with the museums here. How do you expect me to know anyone?'

'You may not know but maybe some of your patients do?'

'Why? What is the matter?'

Ajja repeated the day's happenings and Shekhar became immediately concerned. 'Appa, how could you have allowed Nooni to go out alone with her friends? What if something had happened to her?'

'Nooni is a free spirit and we can't restrict her from going out and exploring the world. Don't be impractical. She loves learning and seeing new things and wants to discover things on her own. Everyone is proud of her here.'

Nooni heard her grandfather talking and took the phone from him. She told her father, 'Dad, stop worrying about me and don't get upset with Ajja. I wasn't alone. I had four friends with me. Spending time here in your village is so much more fun than going to summer classes. I have learnt so much about forests, animals, trees, leaves and birds. I am enjoying every day here. Dad, will you please help Ajja? I'm hoping that our discovery turns out to be a stepwell!'

'What are you talking about? What stepwell?' Shekhar didn't understand a thing.

Ajji grabbed the phone and said, 'Shekhar, you won't understand because you don't believe. If the ruins are indeed a stepwell, then you will realize what Nooni has done for this village. So if you can think of someone and can connect your father to him or her, it would be really nice,' she concluded.

Nooni took the phone back and said, 'Dad, my birthday is coming up this month and I want you to give me a gift. Please don't say no. You don't have to take me to a mall, restaurant or a shop and I don't need dresses, DVDs, toys or books. I only want you to connect us to someone who can help dig up this place as early as possible. You have many friends in Bangalore . . . surely you know someone who can help us. I will never forget this birthday gift. Please, Dad, please!'

Shekhar was speechless and gently said goodbye.

After an hour, he called back and told Nooni, 'I had a patient named Abdul Rasheed and from what I was able to recollect, he heads the Archaeology Department in Bangalore. I called him but he asked me for many details and I didn't know what to tell him. He is a good, knowledgeable man. Here, take down his number. You can contact him and give him all the details he needs. I hope you are happy now, Nooni!'

The Excavation

Somehow, the news spread like wildfire that night and the next morning, many men and women gathered at the site with digging equipment in hand. Shankar Master, who was already at the site, instructed everyone, 'Be very careful. Remove the mud gently. The first task is to make a small path so that we can move around easily and maybe fit in a luggage auto as well.'

The work began in full swing. The sun was getting warmer and soon, it started getting hot.

Meanwhile, Ajji called for a meeting at home with the women of the village. After everyone arrived, she suggested, 'No one is paying the men and women to help with the work at the site. The least we can do is provide them with good food and water. We should give them breakfast, lunch and drinks like buttermilk and tea. If all of you agree with me, I will convert my backyard into a makeshift kitchen. I request you all to come in the morning so that we can divide the work every day. One group can cut the vegetables, another can cook while others can carry the food and distribute it at the site. I want everyone to be involved. The children can give everyone drinking water and collect the garbage. Let's not use plastic plates. I will get some banana leaves from our farm and the workers can eat on them. We will make different things for lunch—around three vegetables and rice, jowar roti and chapatis. Maybe we can restrict the rice so that people don't feel sleepy later while they work.'

Nooni was surprised—Ajji had turned into the commander of an army and was spewing orders to everyone. She seemed to have forgotten about the aches in her knees!

The children decided to separate into two groups—some of them wanted to stay at Ajji's house and help, while others including Nooni and her friends wanted to help at the site.

When Nooni reached the site, she was glad to find everyone happy and excited. The environment was almost festive. Someone had already set up a shamiana and plastic chairs for people to sit. Ajja was the first one to sit there and watch the proceedings keenly. Hanumegowda monitored everyone and Shankar Master came now and then to get Ajja's advice and opinion on the work being done. Amit and a few others were in charge of garbage collection while Nooni was responsible for distributing the water bottles. Medha settled down at a distance and started working on some new sketches.

An hour later, Abdul Rasheed phoned Shankar Master and said, 'It will take a few days to get permission from the state. I have also made a few calls to the central government asking for help. But while the government follows its process, I have decided to come to your village along with four of my assistants so that we can start the work unofficially. The summer season is better for excavation and I want to begin now rather than later when the rainy season is upon us. Unfortunately, we don't have a budget allocated for the project yet. That is my concern.'

Shankar Master handed over the phone to Ajja, who said, 'Please come. We don't want to delay this project under any circumstances. I have an additional house where you and your assistants can stay. We will take complete care of your accommodation and food. But I request you to bring your instruments since we may not have the right tools for you here. If we can help you by escalating this to someone else, let me know so that we can try and talk to them through Hanumegowda. We have already started clearing up the area but we won't excavate or touch anything until your team gets here.'

Abdul Rasheed was pleased with Ajja's answer and promised to come as soon as he could.

Within two days, the workers had removed so much mud that they could see some pillars and steps. A few men created a shelter and Ajji and her team provided dinner and a few Petromax lanterns for the men who stayed back at night to guard the site.

The next morning, Abdul Rasheed drove into Ajja's driveway with a big van and four assistants — two men and two women. Ajja unlocked the house that they used for guests and ensured that it was clean. He offered the place to Abdul and the two men and told the women to stay upstairs in his own house.

That afternoon, the excavation team visited the site. They were surprised to see the interest and help being provided by everyone in the village.

Hanumegowda said, 'We won't be able to help you with money but we can provide you with as many helpers as you need. We will work honestly and to the best of our ability because this site belongs to our village.'

Abdul Rasheed was in his late thirties and had lived in many places in Karnataka because of his transferable job. He was experienced and well-versed in history. He looked around the site and said, 'If you can get more volunteers, then we can finish the job in a short period of time. I am so happy to see the village working as a team. I rarely see such unity in my line of work. Most people think that it is the government's job and disconnect themselves from the project.'

Ajja and Hanumegowda smiled. They were proud of their community and their village.

Then Abdul Rasheed's team started unpacking their tool kits. All the children gathered around them curiously. The team took out a few brushes and some instruments. One of the men began taking measurements while the other started clicking away with his camera. Under their instructions, the workers removed more of the rubble and continued with the same work the entire day.

Later at night during dinner, Ajji asked, 'Rasheed Saheb, what do you think it is—are there any chances of it being a stepwell?'

'No, Amma, I can't tell you for sure—at least not until we have worked for a week. But the monument seems to be untouched and I know that it is going to be a beautiful building.'

For the next few weeks, the workers and Rasheed's team toiled tirelessly. In time, they uncovered more steps and pillars, but the most exciting discovery was that of the small temples between the pillars.

Then the real work began from the top to the bottom—just like any other excavation. The team was keen to see if they would find coins, earthenware, skeletons, gold, inscriptions or copper plates. Coins would indicate the time or era of the construction of the temple. Coins could also give information about the ruler or the wealth of the land. Stone inscriptions would give more details about the temple—when it was built or in whose memory it was constructed.

As they brushed out the details, sixteen pillars were discovered on the first floor. Every pillar was carved out of black stone and was different in design. The polish was so immaculate that it looked like it had been done in recent times — almost like it had been done by a machine.

Shankar Master wondered, 'How did they do such fine polish in those days when there were no machines at all?'

'It is all hand polish,' said one of the women from Rasheed's team. 'In those days, people worked with different techniques that have been long forgotten now. The reason that they spent so much time on it is that money wasn't their only motivation. They thought that they were building something beautiful for God. So they did it with sincerity and devotion.'

Within a few more days, it was clear that the structure was rectangular and opened up to the sky.

'What could this be?' asked Ajja.

'I think it's a well. If it was a complete temple, then it would have definitely had a roof,' said Abdul Rasheed.

The first small temple was in the corner of a large platform and faced eastwards. There were well-laid out steps and hand railings on both sides of the platform. The temple itself was small in size and the name of the deity was written on the top — Chandrashekhara and Shailaja, different names for Lord Shiva and goddess Parvati. Rasheed scanned the script of the letters and concluded that the temple would be at least a thousand years old. The platform moulded into a wall with a running storyline. The first story was of Lord Shiva killing an elephant demon and dancing.

After a few days, the second platform became visible. It had another temple — that of the goddess Saraswati holding a book and a veena. Saraswati was written on the top and there was a pictorial description of her different poses on the wall.

By now, six weeks had passed since Nooni's arrival. Usha was going to be back in Bangalore the next day. She told Nooni on the phone, 'As soon as I reach Bangalore, I'm going to come to Somanahalli and bring you back. I have really missed you.'

Even Shekhar had missed Nooni. He hated the silence in the house after a hard day of work in the hospital.

After Usha reached Bangalore, she called Ajja and Ajji and said, 'Shekhar and I will come to

Somanahalli the day after tomorrow. Will you please make sure that Nooni is ready to leave by then?'

'We will really miss Nooni but I think that you should ask her yourself about when she wants to return. Our village is in the midst of a temple excavation.'

Usha was surprised. 'I thought that there was some minor archaeology work going on. Why is the whole village involved? I would love to see the excavation too!'

Nooni heard everything but didn't know what to tell her parents. She didn't want to go back yet!

After two days, Usha and Shekhar arrived at the village. As usual, Shekhar told his father, 'We are here only for half a day . . . we'll leave in the afternoon.'

Usha hurriedly went to look for Nooni inside the house but couldn't find her anywhere. When she went to Ajji's bedroom, she was startled to see that Nooni had not packed her bags yet. Ajji saw her disappointed face and suggested, 'Why don't you go and see Nooni at the excavation site?'

Both Shekhar and Usha rushed to the site. They were surprised to see the number of activities going on—people were cleaning, fetching water, writing notes and some were gently brushing the statues with soft brushes. The location was very clean and the luggage auto was transporting food.

Finally, Usha saw Nooni — she was very busy collecting garbage and putting it in a plastic bag. When she saw her mother, her face lit up with joy. She quickly washed her face and hands in the water tank nearby and ran towards her mother and hugged her. Usha said happily, 'Nooni, even though I was in Delhi, my mind was always here. I really missed you. I've got you some nice dresses and some quiz books from Delhi. I've also brought some gifts for your friends.'

While talking to Nooni, Usha's eyes fell on the structure and its stunning ornate steps. 'Oh my god!' she exclaimed. 'I never thought that this would be so beautiful.'

'Amma, go talk to Rasheed Uncle. He can tell you a lot more,' Nooni said.

Usha immediately walked across to Abdul Rasheed.

Meanwhile, Shekhar was even more surprised. He had never been able to understand the enthusiasm of discovering something from the past. 'So what if the temple has been buried for a thousand years? Maybe,' he thought, 'all small incidents get a lot of importance in a village. Here, people have more time on their hands than in the city. There is usually no rush to do anything, except maybe getting to school or the post office on time. In such a leisure-based atmosphere, this break from people's routine must have distracted everyone. Where is the time to do all this in a place like Bangalore, where we have to save every minute for work or travel? Besides, the city has become so cosmopolitan that it belongs to everybody and nobody, all at the same time.'

After talking to Usha, Abdul Rasheed came to meet Shekhar. He greeted the doctor and said, 'Sir, I am really touched by your father's generosity. He supplies coconut water to all of us every day and in the afternoon, your mother sends us food and buttermilk. Since the excavation began, none of the cucumbers from your farm have been sold. They've all been used by the people here, who have been toiling with us for weeks now. Your parents are generous to a fault. Thanks to the wonderful people here, we haven't had to hire any security guards. Moreover, this is a good break for me. I have instructed everyone not to inform the media until the excavation is complete, or else reporters will gather here and ask us questions that we don't have answers to yet.'

Shekhar did not know what to say and simply nodded. Then he turned to Nooni. 'Go home and get ready. We have to leave for Bangalore in two hours.'

'No, Dad, I don't want to go back yet. I want to stay until the excavation is complete. Please, I want to see if the water that Ajji talked about in the story is actually there!'

'Nooni, come on, it's just a story!' Then Shekhar asked Rasheed, 'Mr Abdul, how much more time will the excavation take?'

'Around three more weeks.'

'Dad,' Nooni interrupted them, 'I have holidays for four more weeks and I am very happy here. Let me see the complete stepwell and finish my holidays here. I promise I will come back as soon as it is done.'

By then, Usha had also joined them. She put her hand on her husband's arm and said, 'Shekhar, there are so many things about life that you can't learn from books. I think that this experience is one of them. And Nooni has also worked hard for this project. I don't mind staying here for a few days with her.'

Shekhar smiled and gave in to his wife and daughter.

Days later, Abdul Rasheed and his team traced the third temple—of Lord Vishnu with his wife, Lakshmi. Vishnu was sleeping on a serpent and Lakshmi sat near his feet. The temple was called Anantashayana. The story on the platform was a part of the Ramayana.

Soon, the team uncovered the fourth temple. It was a temple of Rama, Lakshmana and Sita, and the storyline described Sita's stay in Ashokavana, the bridge built by the monkey army and Rama's eventual coronation.

The next week, it was the turn of the fifth temple—dedicated to Hanuman. It depicted Hanuman opening up his heart to show Lord Rama residing in it. The story of Hanuman's childhood and how he flew to the sun god to eat him appeared in the corridor.

The sixth temple belonged to sixteen-handed Durga in the act of killing the demon Mahishasur, while the platform told the story of Durga and Parvati.

Lord Ganesha was in a dancing pose in the seventh temple. He had a big stomach and was holding laddoos in one hand while the second one carried a book. His other two hands held weapons. Accordingly, his story lined the platform.

The last temple had the statue of the goddess Ganga. She held a big pot in her hand. Along the platform was the story of the churning of the sea, and at the bottom of the well there was a cow's face.

That night, Ajja developed high fever and was unable to get out of bed. Ajji gave him some home remedies but they didn't help. Ajji advised him not to go to the site the next morning. Ajja refused to listen to her and somehow made his way there. But Abdul Rasheed sent him back. The fever continued for days and Ajji became very concerned. She called up her son. 'Shekhar, your father has high fever for the last three days. I want to take him to the hospital in the town nearby. What medicine should I give him?'

'Amma, first have his blood tested to see if it is a viral infection or not. These days, Bangalore has all sorts of diseases like swine flu, chikungunya and dengue fever. I don't want to scare you, it is better to start treatment early for him since he is old. He must come here to Bangalore so I can take good care of him.'

Ajja came on the line and refused outright. 'I can't travel in this state. Why can't you come here tomorrow?'

'Appa, I have some patients to take care of.'

Ajji took the phone from Ajja and said, 'If you have patients then you must also have assistants. This is your father, for god's sake. Come here and examine him.'

Shekhar reached Somanahalli by mid-morning the next day. Once he was there, he found that many people in the village were displaying the same symptoms as Ajja. So he distributed whatever medicine he had to as many people as he could.

He asked his mother, 'What happened to the primary health centre here?'

Ajji said, 'The doctor there has gone on vacation. There is nobody here whom we can run to in times of crisis. I request you—please come to the village regularly and take care of people like us. You come from this village too and you can understand the people here. Think about it. You will be doing us a great service.'

Shekhar did not say anything and left for Bangalore.

By now, two and a half weeks had already passed

and the structure was ready for viewing. There were eight beautiful temples in all and twenty-one steps from the ground to the bottom of the well. But there was no water in the pond—this was a stepwell without water. So everyone came to the conclusion that whatever they had heard about the stepwell was true, except for one small difference. There were eight small shrines and not all of them were of Lord Shiva.

Nooni asked Abdul Rasheed, 'Amma says that Lord Ganesha is always first when it comes to initiating anything new or special. He is worshipped before any other god. Then why is he at the bottom of the stepwell in this case? Shouldn't he be on the top?'

'No,' he replied. 'Since the water source is at the bottom, the water will touch Ganapati first.'

Nooni nodded. She finally understood the logic behind placing Lord Ganesha where he was.

There were many inscriptions on the steps and the walls of the structure. Abdul Rasheed translated the script loudly for everyone to hear.

This great stepwell temple is built by King Somanayaka in 1000 CE (Hindu calendar date 922 of Shalivahana Saka). Somanayaka believes in all Gods. He has built this temple in the memory of his late father who died in battle with the Ganga dynasty. The temple has taken ten years to build with the cooperation of the best artisans in the land.

This stepwell should be used only for the purpose of obtaining drinking water and on full moon nights, the temple must be kept closed for repair and maintenance.

Somanayaka has donated hundreds of acres of lands to several people. The entire stretch of land has been divided into seven equal parts. The first part belongs to the main priest and his family who performs the puja at the temple several times a day. The second portion is donated to the man who looks after the administration and maintenance of the temple and also works as an assistant to the main priest. He can be from any community. The third portion goes to the person who cleans the temple every day. The fourth part is for the person who brings flowers and makes garlands for all the deities. The fifth is for the person who lights the lamps of the temple in the name of the king. The sixth portion is reserved for the dancers and musicians of the temple who perform their art in front of the gods. The seventh and the last is for the cooking and distribution of food to the pilgrims.

If someone takes over the property and does not do their duty, then they must return the property or else be subject to punishment.

King Somanayaka has proclaimed, "If somebody helps in restoration of this temple in due course of time, then I will be grateful to them—no matter what community they are from—because they would have understood my spirit. I will touch their feet from wherever I am. I pray for such people to increase their population on Mother Earth."'

While everyone was happy to see the structure, Ajja and Ajji were not. They were really concerned about the lack of water. According to them, a well without water was like a tree without leaves, a sky without the sun and a night without the moon and the stars.

'Why was this temple closed?' A question echoed from the visitors.

'Logically, I can tell you why but I'm not sure if it's the right explanation,' said Abdul Rasheed. 'The temple and the statues are intact, which means that there was no foreign invasion here. I think that there was a war and at the time, this temple must have been very famous. The king might have been scared that his enemies would destroy the temple and so, he covered it up with sand to avoid spoiling the artefacts inside. Cleverly, he covered the top of the well with mud to hide it completely. It was his way of protecting the structure. He must have planned to reopen the temple after his enemies retreated. But maybe that never happened because he lost the battle. Over a period of time, this incident became a story and as it got passed down from generation to generation, it became less and less accurate. That would explain the different folk stories about the stepwell.'

'What about the water? The source must be really close to this.'

'I believe that it should be somewhere near the cow's mouth because here in India, we believe that a source of water must be directed in such a way that it flows through a cow. Let's do some work near the cow's mouth tomorrow and remove all the dirt from the pond. Maybe we can disassemble the cow and see where the block is.'

By noon the next day, all the women from the village came to the site with a pot in hand. They were hopeful about finding the source of water. When Abdul Rasheed disassembled the cow's face, they saw a huge stone kept against an opening, presumably to stop the flow of water. Abdul was right! He explained, 'Somanayaka's architect must have advised him to close the source of water before shutting the well completely. That was sensible.

Without the water, the well became dry and it was easy for them to fill it with sand and mud.'

The team cleaned the area around the source of water and removed the stone carefully. At first, the water was slow and muddy but within minutes, it became clear. Within a few hours, the water reached the bottom step of the well.

One of the women wanted to drink the water and brought the pot close to the bottom of the well. Immediately, Ajji said, 'Stop! Let's not drink any water before praying to the goddess Ganga, who is the mother of all rivers. Let's thank her for being here. Give the first glass of water to Rasheed Saheb. He has done so much work for our temple.'

Ajji grabbed a steel tumbler, filled it with water and offered it to Abdul Rasheed. He faced eastwards to Mecca, did a quick namaz and prayed, 'O Allah! Be merciful on us and on this temple and these people. Let the water here be a source of energy and inspiration. Let it flow in abundance without any constraints.'

Then he drank the water and said, 'It is as sweet as coconut water.'

Ajji opened a cane basket lying on a chair by her side. There were many things inside it—a sari, a blouse, bangles, flowers, a bowl of kumkum, fruits, a box of mithai, coconut and ration for one person's lunch. She kept the basket in front of the goddess Ganga, touched it to the cow's head and turned to Rasheed, 'In Karnataka, we call this *marada bagina*. It is given as an offering. I take goddess Ganga's blessings and give it to your wife. This is our tradition and I hope that you will accept it, Rasheed Saheb.'

Abdul Rasheed was speechless. He bowed down humbly and took the basket.

The next tumbler of water was for Nooni. Suddenly, she was nowhere to be found. Ever since the excavation had started, she was always helping in some way. Everyone was aware that it was this little girl's strong will that had helped locate the stepwell. Nooni was called and she came running from the back of the site. Though the water was neither boiled nor cooled, she drank without hesitation.

Shankar Master added, 'This is pure water from the spring and passes through sand, which means that natural filtration has taken place.'

'Oh, it is sweeter than nectar!' Nooni repeated the lines from Ajji's story.

Everybody rejoiced and one by one, all the women took a tumbler of water.

That evening, the press was also informed and soon, reporters started coming in.

Initially, Abdul Rasheed had not entertained them. But now, he felt that the time had come for the country to know about their discovery.

Hordes of people started interviewing Ajja, Hanumegowda, Shankar Master and Abdul Rasheed and his team. But nobody forgot little Nooni and her band of friends. Everybody asked the same question—'What made you boys and girls dig that day?'

All the children felt shy and hesitated to answer the reporters' questions but not Nooni. She boldly said, 'Anyone who loves our village and believed in the existence of a stepwell would have done the same.'

Ajja thought that it was a very diplomatic answer.

Shekhar was also interviewed.

Within a day, the news of the excavation hit the daily newspaper of the state. Lots of photographs appeared in the media. Some enthusiastic volunteers also made a small guidebook for the structure. The Minister of Culture declared, 'This is a state heritage site now and there will be a special bus from Bangalore to make it easier for visitors to get there.'

The news reached Delhi and even the central minister for education showed an interest in giving the stepwell a special grant and allocating a budget.

Soon, a new sign was painted at the entrance of Somanahalli, along with a small write-up about Somanayaka and his deeds. The sign read—'Please visit the beautiful stepwell architecture of the village.'

It was a wonderful time.

A Send-off Party

The next day was Friday and almost the end of Nooni's ten-week holiday. Her school was to start on Monday. Amit was going to leave in two days for Delhi while Medha and Anand were moving on to the next grade in Varada High School in the village. Mahadeva was also going to start his daily journey to Haveri to continue his studies.

It was time to get back to each one's routine.

Nooni was supposed to leave the village in the afternoon the next day. Her father was coming to pick her up. In the evening, she began gathering her clothes and packing her bags. Ajji was sad. Her granddaughter had stayed with her for ten long weeks and had brought new enthusiasm to their old age. She was going to miss her.

Nooni, on the other hand, felt like she had learnt

a lot. She had made new friends from different backgrounds and their friendship was healthy and uncompetitive. Thanks to her father's dictionary, her Kannada vocabulary was better now. She had learnt the joy of making papads, giving water to everyone and living with nature and fresh air, but she was yet to learn more about birds, trees, plants and insects. The most important thing of them all was that she could now cycle on her own everywhere. Last, but not the least, she was proud of playing a vital role in the excavation of the famous stepwell of Somanahalli.

Then Ajja had an idea. He decided to honour the forty volunteers who had worked on the project. Initially, many people had joined the excavation but the numbers had slowly dropped because of various reasons. These forty men and women had stayed on till the end. It was easy to honour the head of the institution or the person-in-charge, but most people forgot about those who execute the work. Without their contribution, the whole project would not have worked.

Ajja called up his son. 'Shekhar, when you come tomorrow, please bring two baskets of apples and forty watches, out of which twenty-five must be for men and fifteen for women.'

'I will do as you wish but what is going on, Appa?'

'I am arranging a send-off lunch for everyone involved with the project and I want to give the volunteers a token of appreciation too.'

Shekhar was surprised. 'Who is going to cook? Amma?'

'You don't worry about the logistics. I have hired two cooks from Haveri.'

'Okay,' said Shekhar, as he said goodbye and disconnected the call.

The next day, the weather was cool and pleasant. It was the end of summer and the beginning of the rainy season. There was a huge pandal near the stepwell. The tables were laid and banana leaves were spread out. The meal was excellent.

After lunch, a small stage was set up for Ajja, Hanumegowda, Abdul Rasheed and Shankar Master. By then, Shekhar had also reached the site and stood at the side.

Everyone else sat down in front of the stage.

Hanumegowda began his speech, 'Dear fellow villagers, we are very proud that this day has arrived. It has come with the effort of many people. Shankar Master has told us many potential reasons for the closure of the well. But at the end of the day, one detail remains common—people disrespected the water source. The story of Ratnavati indicates that she swam here and contaminated the water, while the story of Shashi Shekhara says that he had a party here and spoiled the water. And once water is contaminated, it becomes a haven for diseases. So we must respect the source.'

'How do we stop the contamination from happening?' asked someone from the audience.

'On behalf of the panchayat, we are planning to impose some rules here,' replied Hanumegowda. 'We will build another area for people to wash their feet before entering the stepwell. No one will carry more than one pot of water from the well and it will be used solely for drinking. No one is allowed to swim or have picnics here. But we will leave it open for activities such as music and dance, and the audience is welcome to sit and watch. Let's not dirty the premises by breaking coconuts or leaving food as an offering to the gods, which will only lead to crows and insects gathering here. Every day, a priest will come and perform the puja and people are welcome to come and visit the temple.'

Hanumegowda took a deep breath and continued, 'I will arrange for an office counter outside. I know that people like to gift saris, coins, blouses or bangles to Ganga Mata and throw these things in the water, but it will be forbidden here. Instead, they can deposit their offerings at the counter. Then we will hold an annual auction for the offerings such as saris and the money we receive will be used for the maintenance of the temple. We will not ask the government for money. This is our stepwell and we should take care of it.'

Next, Ajja stood up and thanked everyone closely associated with the success of the project. He said firmly, 'Let us keep the tradition of keeping the stepwell premises closed twice a month on full moon days. Since all of you have been an integral part of this endeavour, I would like to honour everyone present here today. I would like to call these five people on stage to help us do that. Nooni, Amit, Anand, Medha and Mahadeva, please come here.'

Everyone was pleasantly surprised and they clapped with great gusto.

It was a joyous occasion.

After the volunteers had returned to their seats, Abdul Rasheed said, 'This is an unusual experience for me. I will try to get funding from the state and central governments for a garden and boundary wall surrounding the stepwell.'

Shankar Master stood up to say a vote of thanks, but Shekhar requested him to allow him to speak. Shankar Master nodded and sat down again.

Shekhar stood where he was and turned to look at the audience. 'I know that I am not on stage, but I would like to say something. I have decided to make a two-day trip to the village every month. Appa can convert one of his houses to a small clinic suitable for outpatients and I will give free treatment to everyone. I belong to this village and I must give back to my people here.'

Then he looked at Mahadeva. 'I will also provide capital money towards Mahadeva's project but only after he completes his graduation. He is bright and brave and has been a tremendous source of strength to Nooni during her stay here. Our village needs more people like Hanumegowda and Mahadeva.'

Everyone clapped with joy upon hearing Shekhar's plans. After a while, everyone returned to their homes.

Once Nooni reached Ajja and Ajji's home, she picked up her bags and Shekhar kept them in the car. Then he turned to his parents and said, 'Appa and Amma, I think that the wisest decision Usha and I ever made was to send Nooni here. I know that she has missed some competitive classes but I have realized the importance of giving one's child the opportunity for overall development. Nooni has taught me that and I am privileged to belong to this village.'

Then he turned to his daughter and said, 'Nooni, I was becoming like most parents who want nothing more than their children to perform brilliantly in academics. I had forgotten about how important it is for you to experience all that life has to offer. Today, with all that you have done and learnt, I feel like you have come first in your class. I can't tell you how proud I am to have you as my daughter.'

'I am very happy,' said Ajji with a smile on her face. 'Nooni was able to do what Usha and I couldn't.'

As Nooni walked out the front door, she saw many villagers gathered around to say goodbye. Somehow, she had become a part of their lives.

Nooni handed over the gifts her mother had brought from Delhi to Medha, Amit and Mahadeva. She gave two cross-stitch kits to Medha. Medha also gave her a purse that she herself had knitted. Quietly, she said, 'Nooni, I have made this for you. Think of me whenever you use this purse.'

Ajji asked Mahadeva to put a big bag of papads, bottles of pickles, heaps of laddoos and bunches of bananas in the car. She told her son, 'These papads were rolled by me but some were baked and watched over by Nooni so they are hers. She was my right hand running around the kitchen as I made the mango pickle. I will really miss her.'

Then Ajji gave Nooni a traditional pearl necklace and said, 'This is my gift to you. When I was your age, my grandmother handed this down to me. I want you to have it and treasure it. It's yours to keep forever.'

Nooni put her arm around Ajji and whispered in her ear, 'I am happy about the gift but what I really want is a toilet near the Varada river and Varada Hill. Children like me visit these places often and it's very sad that there are no toilets for them there.'

Ajji laughed loudly. 'You don't have to whisper, Nooni. I will consider this my next task and ensure that our entire village takes responsibility for it. By the time you visit us next, we will have a few toilets in both the areas. I promise.'

Nooni hugged Ajji. She looked at her face and saw the tears in her eyes. Nooni said, 'Don't worry, Ajji. I will come here every year. I like to spend my holidays with you.'

Ajja, however, did not say much. He was very proud of his granddaughter's achievement. Gently, he placed his hand on her head and patted her.